I0570878

HARLAN'S FATED

Creekside Township Rivals

Book 5

JT Fader

This book is a work of fiction. The characters, incidences, and dialogue are drawn from the author's imagination and are not to be construed as real. Any resemblance to actual events or persons, living or dead, is entirely coincidental.

HARLAN'S FATED Copyright © 2024 by JT Fader (Leigh Jarrett). All rights reserved. No part of this book may be used or reproduced in any manner whatsoever without written permission, except in the case of brief quotations embodied in critical articles and reviews. All trademarks are the property of the respective owners.

Published by Steambath Press
A Creekside Township Rivals Romance

Paperback published March 2024
ISBN-13: 978-1-998008-51-3

Chapter One | Harlan

I couldn't get used to it—working without my brother, Reese. Ever since his accident with a leg hold trap when he'd lost his hand, I'd been running our plumbing business on my own. I missed the banter and the ease we had with each other. The camaraderie of brothers.

From the time I was sixteen, I'd been working with Reese. Starting the day after my sire and carrier had decided because I had reached shifting age, I was old enough to fend for myself.

I hadn't been. I'd been dropped off with Reese while my protectors from the time I was whelped took off for more excitement away from sleepy Creekside Township. Reese had become like a new sire to me. Taming my wanton need to run off into the forest with my friends to harass game once I shifted to wolf form again for the first time. And teaching me how to be an adult wolf.

Even though Reese was an Omega, and I was an Alpha, I relied on him to guide me. He watched out for me. I loved him for it. Being essentially abandoned as a teenager had caused some deep wounds. Reese had been there for me as I worked through the hurt and anger.

Three years later, not even twenty, I had the entire responsibility of *Armstrong Plumbing* on my shoulders. Reese had called me this morning to discuss changing the direction of the business.

I feared I knew where the discussion would lead.

Right now, first things first, I had a brutal headache, and I was hungry. I'd slept off a crazy night out with my friends. We'd closed out the only bar in Creekside last night. I'd stumbled home, barely able to make it up the driveway, all alone, because all three of my best friends lived off the wolf compound. We'd gone to high school together. We frequently tore up the town.

I started with aspirin, then I followed the scent of fresh venison wafting up the stairs. Carina must have been out at dawn hunting down some game with her mate, Kal.

I jogged down the stairs into the kitchen. She'd set out plates on the table with sizeable chunks of meat on each. Two other wolves from our house were already growling and snarling and snapping at each other as they fed. I slid into an empty chair, saw red, and tore into the tender flesh. I had to protect my plate, using my elbows to keep the much larger wolves to either side of me away.

I had yet to fill out fully. I was as muscular as I could be for a nineteen-year-old wolf, but my body hadn't been through my final development where I would look like an adult Alpha male.

I'd been told, I certainly had the attitude of one.

I finished my meat and used one of the warm cloths on the table to clean myself. Sometimes my confidence got me into trouble. I'd squared off with every wolf in our house at some point or another. It could be something as simple as who was next in the shower. The larger wolves tried to bully me out of the way and place me at the end of the queue.

I wouldn't hear of it.

Not sure if they were afraid of my crazy or if I simply amused them, but after a brief confrontation, they would laugh at me and let me keep my place.

"Are you heading over to Reese and Mark's?" Carina asked.

"Yeah, they want to talk to me about the business."

"Try to keep an open mind."

"You know what they're going to propose, don't you?"

"I do. Mark and I talked it over."

I grunted and sighed. I knew too. Or at least I suspected. There was no point in having two plumbing businesses in Creekside. *Armstrong Plumbing* was going to be no more.

I went back upstairs to grab a hoody. The spring weather was upon us, but it was still chilly in the morning. My gaze landed on the second bed in my room. Reese and I had shared a bedroom for almost three years. He'd moved out when he met his fated mate, Peter.

Losing Peter had been devastating for the entire pack. Listening to Reese's howls of anguish each night had nearly broken every single one of us. We'd tried to offer our support, but Reese had wanted to be left alone. He needed to mourn at his own speed without the help of his pack.

Finding Mark so soon after losing Peter had surprised us all. Especially because Mark was the leader of the Riverton pack. We were even more surprised when Mark gave up his leadership and his pack to be with Reese. To become his mate. Of course, we had welcomed him.

He kept Reese basking in happiness and love.

And Mark was amazing with little Peter. He treated him as if he were his own pup. I often saw Mark taking Peter for a walk, bundled to his chest. Or in town, the same—giving Reese a much-needed break. He loved his new family. That much was obvious.

What wasn't so obvious was how Mark felt about leaving his pack. He didn't like to talk about it. His pack's strict traditions had made it impossible for him to choose otherwise.

I wasn't sure if I could ever do that—leave my pack for a wolf. He would have to be my fated mate. And we'd need to be in love. Even then, the idea churned up my stomach.

I was loyal to the pack of my birth. Fiercely so. While I was still in school, I'd ended up in many fights with wolves from West Creekside. They didn't have a school of their own. Our pack, East Creekside had Creekside Township within its territory. West Creekside had nothing but forest. They owned businesses in town. Mainly auto mechanical shops. Trucks, cars, and motorbikes. Towing. And their leader Carl was now the Sheriff of Creekside Township.

Lucas had considered the position of Sheriff when it first came open but felt it would impact his family time. Their family had achieved a capacity of 12. There didn't appear to be more coming. Adam had passed through his usual time of becoming pregnant and he hadn't. Our leader had enough on his hands without adding Sheriff to his job list.

I trudged up the steps to Reese's house and knocked on the door.

I was met by my rather tired looking brother. He looked to be more than 13 years older than me. I reached down and picked up little Peter who was dancing around Reese's feet.

"You look terrible," I said to Reese.

Reese laughed. "Thanks. Mark Jr. isn't sleeping well. Not sure if it's because he's an Alpha, but he feeds more often than Peter ever did."

"You not getting enough sleep?"

"Not by a long shot. Mark takes care of them when he gets home from work so I can sleep for a couple of hours. And he takes one of the overnight feedings. Even with that—I'm exhausted."

"If Mark is ever working late, let me know. I'll cover for you so you can get some sleep."

Reese smiled. It was an action that lessened the serious look on his face. A look I shared. You could tell instantly we were brothers. We both took after our sire. Thick dark hair, dark stern features, and pale blue eyes that always caught the attention of interested male wolves.

Mark Jr. had a grey and brown coat like his sire, but he'd inherited the blue eyes from Reese. He was a perfect blend of them both. At two weeks old, he'd only just opened his eyes.

"I appreciate that, Harlan," Reese replied. "I will be holding you to it."

"Wouldn't have offered if I didn't mean it." I listened for Mark. There was rustling happening out in the carport. "Mark wanted to talk to me?" I rubbed Peter's head and set him down.

"He'll be back in a second. He's organizing some supplies for his next job."

"It's about winding down *Armstrong Plumbing*, isn't it?"

"It's what's best for the pack."

The door to the carport slammed shut and Mark plodded down the hall. He was an immense wolf. To be honest, he scared me a little. If he wasn't such a softy, Lucas ought to be concerned. Also, Mark had played on repeat that he wasn't interested in leading a pack again.

"Glad you're here, Harlan," Mark said.

"Sounded important."

"It is." Mark walked toward the living room. "Let's sit."

I took a seat on a chair across from the sofa Mark and Reese were settling into. I crossed and uncrossed my arms, unsure how to present myself. I felt like a child about to lose their toy.

Mark leaned forward and clasped his hands together. "Lucas and I think it's best if there is only one plumbing company in Creekside."

Even though I suspected it was going to happen, I could feel my chest deflate. I wanted to argue my case to keep what my brother and I had built alive, but I knew it was pointless. Mark was right. There was no point in us competing against one another.

I stared into Mark's kindly brown eyes. "Then what happens to me?"

"I'd like you to join *Cooper Plumbing*. To come work for me."

Now, I absolutely crossed my arms. "As an equal partner."

"I was thinking as an employee."

I shook my head. "No. I have a loyal customer base, my own truck, and my own tools. You can't possibly have acquired enough customers yet to keep you afloat. You need me."

"Those customers of yours would come to me eventually."

"I've already built rapport with them. They trust me. You don't honestly think someone isn't going to fill your boots over in Riverton and start their own plumbing business and try to undercut yours for business in Creekside? Like I said already—you need me."

Mark grunted. "Your brother warned me you'd counter my offer."

"I could just as easily apprentice with someone in a different trade. Maybe Lucas is looking for more electricians to join his business."

Mark raised his hands. "All right. All right. An employee with a share of the profit."

I jumped to my feet. "I'm going to leave if you keep this up." Not sure where I got the courage from, but I wasn't backing down. I wasn't going from owning my own business to being an employee for someone else. I wanted a full share of the profits. Not a wage plus a pittance.

"70/30," Mark said.

"50/50."

"60/40."

I growled and let my canines descend. "50. 50."

Mark grunted again. "Okay, but only because you're Reese's brother. I expect you to work as hard as I do. Not just take half the profits. There was never much work in Riverton so I'm looking forward to expanding the business. Your contacts better be sound."

Of course, they were. Reese and I had been professional and reliable.

Mark rose and extended his hand. "Do we have a deal?"

I shook Mark's hand. "Let me know when the paperwork is done."

"I think Mark was hoping you'd help him today," Reese said.

"I have my own job today. Once the paperwork is signed, we can talk about working on jobs together. Until then, *Armstrong Plumbing* is still an entity."

Mark smiled at me. It made me smirk. You couldn't help but love the wolf. Even though he sometimes scared me, I knew deep down he was a cinnamon roll—all gooey and warm inside.

"Friday at the latest," Mark said. "I'll contact my lawyer today."

"If everything is in order, I'll start working with you on Monday."

Mark laughed and crossed his arms. "You have the makings of a formidable Alpha."

I cocked an eyebrow at him. "Already am."

Mark coughed and chuckled. "Go to work. I'll deliver the paperwork to you."

I leaned down and ruffled Peter's fur. "Bye, little wolf." Reese swept in as Peter barked and growled at me in a burst of energy. He caught him before he attacked my pant leg.

"Sorry, he's going through a biting phase," Reese said as he lifted Peter in one hand.

"He'll be a fierce Omega like his Papa," Mark said.

Reese leaned against Mark and kissed his cheek. "I'm hardly fierce. I'm just tired." Mark Jr. yawned from within the folds of the pup carrier strapped to Reese's chest. "And he's awake again."

"I'll leave you to it." I rubbed Reese's arm. "Remember what I said about pupsitting."

"Be prepared for a call," Reese shouted to me as I made my way down their front steps. I waved at him and jogged to my truck out front of Carina's house.

This morning's job was going to be easy. The homeowner wanted the garburator removed from their kitchen and they needed me to check for the source of a leak beneath their washing machine. It was a stacked combo inside a closet. It was going to take some muscle.

It was a human customer, I'd worked for them many times before, replacing faucets and toilets, and last month installing a new dishwasher. I usually dealt with the wife, Linda.

That's who was waiting for me as I approached the house. Linda drank. I could always tell when she was the only one in the house by the scent of scotch or gin.

The front door popped open after I rang the doorbell.

"Harlan, how nice to see you again," Linda said and patted my cheek. Linda was also handsy, but she was a dream to work for. She knew exactly what she wanted but also what was feasible. She never asked me for the impossible.

"You too. Let's get this garburator out." I headed straight for the kitchen with my assortment of tools. She hovered as I opened the cabinet under the sink and started the job. Once it was out and I'd replaced the necessary pipes, I changed the switch on the wall to a flat immovable plate.

"So glad to see that beast gone," she said, rubbing my shoulder.

"Yeah, they're not allowed to put them in houses anymore. Hard on the sewer system."

"Can I make you a coffee?"

"That would be amazing. Thank you."

The laundry appliances were in the mud room. Once I had access to the base of the washing machine, Linda brought me my coffee. I took a seat on the bench to drink it.

"So, tell me, Harlan, do you have a girlfriend yet?"

I laughed. "You asked me that last time I was here."

"That was three months ago. Surely you've met a nice she-wolf."

I snorted. "I'd be looking for a female Omega. Not a she-wolf."

"Right. Right. You told me that. I can never get the lingo right."

"Plus, like I told you, I wouldn't be looking for a female."

"Oh, that's right … you're gay."

I didn't have the heart to correct her again. *Gay* wasn't a word used in wolf vocabulary. You either preferred females or males. Any pairing could produce pups. Except for two Alpha males, two Omegas males, or two females, all of which were frowned upon in most packs. Lucas was progressive in that respect. Our pack was producing so many pups, he was open to any combination of wolf relationships.

Bryant, Grayson, and Hunter were a good example. The polyamorous relationship worked for them. They were in love and the East Creekside pack had accepted them.

"I'm too young to be looking for a mate. I don't turn twenty for another 6 months."

"That's a shame. You should be out there having fun."

I finished my coffee. "Trust me, I'm having fun. Maybe too much."

Linda squeezed my shoulder and took my cup. "No such thing. A cutie like you must be attracting the attention of many male wolves."

I smirked. "Not so far." And that was the truth. Every available *gay* Omega wolf I knew was part of my friend group which meant they were off-limits.

It was embarrassing, but I'd never even kissed anyone.

Unless you counted the time my friend Damon and I were so drunk we found ourselves clinging to each other on the bleachers at the school sports field one night.

We'd shared breath, lips barely touching—then burst out laughing and pulled away, nearly falling off our seats onto the grass. It had never happened again.

We'd never talked about it.

And that was the extent of my love life.

Chapter Two | Logan

The further south I traveled, the taller the trees became and the greener the forest. I'd been padding through the forest for over a month, moving toward what I hoped would be a new life.

I was headed for Creekside where I'd heard packs were thriving and looking for new members. I knew no one, but it was a chance I was willing to take. I needed to run far away from my past.

My pack leader had *encouraged* me to leave as there was no resolving the issues that had arisen over the years. I'd been told I was delusional, and I'd brought on what had happened to me.

I refused to believe either of those things.

I'd never considered myself weak. I wasn't large for an Alpha, but I could usually hold my own. My one and only mate had torn down that illusion. We'd met during a pack hunt. He was a new Omega to the pack and looking for an Alpha to mate and have pups with.

We'd hunted well together. At first, he hadn't been interested in mating with me, but then we'd become friends. I wouldn't say we fell in love but there was certainly affection there.

We'd tried through three of his heat cycles but hadn't produced a pup. He became angry with me, throwing my truth in my face. We'd argued a lot and then he'd become violent.

My Omega matched me in stature. He used to throw that in my face, telling me I wasn't a real Alpha. That a real Alpha would have put a pup in him.

He'd called me an imposter.

We'd taken that fight and many more out into the front pasture, attacking and ripping at each other. My Omega always won the upper hand, which increased his verbal abuse of me.

It was an act of self-preservation—*running away*. Not only had my Omega ridiculed me, but the rest of the pack had also joined in, taunting me, and hollering at me to leave.

They didn't understand. Despite my Omega scent, I knew I was an Alpha. I believed that right down to my very soul. While growing up, my sire had no time for male Omegas, so I'd done everything I could to prove to him I wasn't one, but he'd never accepted me.

He'd never believed I was an Alpha.

I didn't want to be seen as an Omega. That meant submitting to an Alpha which I refused to do. I'd ignored the times of the year I felt like rutting—opening myself up to an Alpha. I had almost convinced myself I was simply an Alpha in rut, looking for a mate.

I knew the truth, but I rejected it.

I wanted to live my life as an Alpha.

Deep down, I *knew* I was an Alpha.

I trotted into a territory that had been claimed by a pack. Another few hours and the pack would be able to pick up my scent. I had deliberately stayed on the west side of the creek. One township north, I'd been told the West Creekside pack were mechanics in Creekside. That fitted with my trade. I restored and repaired motorcycles. I was good at it—and I had proven myself.

Hours later, I caught the scent of a pack scouting group running toward me. Four immense wolves surrounded me. I took a non-threatening position, crouching close to the ground.

One wolf plodded toward me; teeth bared. I whined and rolled onto my side.

I wasn't looking for a fight.

The wolf before me shifted. He was a muscular wolf, around my age of almost 40. Whereas I had dark hair, his was salt and pepper, grey at the temples.

I shifted to speak to him.

"You're on West Creekside pack territory," he said.

"I know. That was my intention."

The other three wolves shifted. One male snickered. "You have a death wish?"

The lead wolf growled over his shoulder at him, then turned back to me.

"What's your business?"

"I'd like to join your pack if you have room for me."

His eyes narrowed. "What's your trade?"

"Motorcycle mechanic."

He nodded. "Patrick and Tyler would appreciate the help. It's not their specialty."

"There's no one else in town?"

"No, folks have to go to Riverton with their motorcycles."

"I have over twenty years of experience."

The lead wolf crossed his arms. "Where are you coming from?"

"The Stoney Hills pack. Up in the tundra."

"Why did you leave?"

I'd given this some thought. I couldn't tell a prospective pack that I'd essentially been run out because the leader disagreed with where in the pack I saw myself.

"Lack of suitable mates."

"Long way to travel to find a mate."

"I needed some time to myself, and I heard you were looking for members."

"You're too old for bearing pups. Our Alphas may not want you."

I looked at my calloused hands. "Yes, I know."

He grunted. "Anything you're not telling me?"

I kept my expression flat. "No, just looking for a fresh start."

"Okay, I'll let our pack leader know. He'll want to talk to you before we accept you."

"Of course." I bowed to the wolf. "Alpha."

"Omega."

The sensation of light fingers crawled up my spine. Despite how much it hurt me, I wasn't going to lose another pack by objecting to being called Omega.

I wouldn't be raising my voice here.

"Follow us."

All four wolves shifted to wolf form. I joined them and took off running through the forest behind them. By the time we reached their compound, the sun was setting.

"Let's get you some clothes," the lead wolf said to me after we shifted on the front porch of a large log home. I followed him into the house. I caught the scent of Alphas, Betas, and Omegas, including a few pups. There was a commotion happening in the kitchen, laughter, and friendly teasing. We were headed in the opposite direction, down a hall, and into a laundry room.

A pair of jeans, a plaid shirt, socks, and boots were thrust at me.

"Put these on."

The clothes were big on me but soft from the dryer. After dressing, I hopped around and pulled on the boots as the wolf clothed himself beside me. "I didn't catch your name."

"You can call me Dan."

I extended my hand. "Dan, I'm Logan."

Dan grunted but took my hand and shook it. "Let's go. Carl is waiting."

"Carl?"

"Our pack leader."

I chased Dan along the hallway and down the front steps of the house. "Of course." We walked a short distance up the driveway until we came to another large log home.

Without knocking, Dan let himself inside. The house smelled of fresh venison and berries. It reminded me that I hadn't fed in almost a week. My stomach growled.

"We'll get you something to eat as soon as we're done," Dan said to me.

"Thank you."

The kitchen we walked into was warm and cozy with caramel-colored wood cabinets and countertops. In front of the large white farm sink was a wolf the size of none I had ever seen before.

He was washing dishes.

"So, you're Logan," he said without turning around.

"Yes, Alpha."

"And you want to join our pack."

"Yes, Alpha."

"How old are you?"

"Thirty-nine."

"You're past your breeding age."

"Yes, Alpha."

"Perhaps you can be useful in other ways. Danny says you're a motorcycle mechanic."

"Yes, restorations and repairs."

"Patrick and Tyler will be keen to have you onboard. Keep business in Creekside."

"I have lots of experience. I won't let them down."

"They're a handful but they run a successful business." Carl finished drying and storing the last dish and then turned to face me. "There's a room with an extra bed at Danny's. You can have it but you're on probation. Let's see where we are in 3 months."

I leaned forward and offered him my hand. "Thank you so much."

My hand practically disappeared in his.

"Welcome, Logan."

I backed away after a firm shake and bowed my head. "Alpha."

"Omega."

I didn't let the term bother me this time. I had a new pack, and I wasn't going to do anything to ruin the opportunity. Maybe in three months, they'd let me into the telepathic link.

The room Dan showed me in his house had three twin beds. It was explained by a helpful Beta that it was a room of male Omegas and that they'd help me secure some more clothes.

After a late feeding, I went upstairs to the room and climbed into bed. I was exhausted. I didn't even hear my roommates come in. And when I woke in the morning, they were gone.

On my bedside table, a phone number for Patrick.

I found the office downstairs where I located the phone. I didn't sit—just dialed the number. It rang for a long time before anyone picked up.

"Creekside Service."

"Hi … um … this is Logan. I found your number on my bedside table."

"Yeah, you were passed out. Didn't want to wake you."

"Do you live in Dan's house?"

"Dude, we share a room with you."

I suppose that was handy. I could get a ride with them to work every day. I would get to know them if we shared a room and sat to feed together.

"Didn't hear a thing last night."

"Danny said you came from a fair distance away."

"Been traveling for over a month."

"And you work with motorcycles?"

"Foreign and domestic. Over twenty years."

"You're going to be a huge asset. We've been losing business to Riverton."

"When do you want me to start?"

"Tyler will head up to the house and pick you up. You can take a look around the shop."

"Sounds good."

"He'll be there in twenty minutes."

"Perfect."

The line went dead. I was already showered and dressed. I just needed some coffee. A delicacy after being in wolf form for a month. I found a fresh pot brewing in the kitchen.

An Omega wolf swept into the room. He was delicate for a wolf. He extended his hand to me. "I'm Marco. Carl's mate. Help yourself to anything you want."

Marco's hand was light in mine, barely a handshake. I was struck by the shade of green staring back at me. Marco was beautiful. His high cheekbones were accentuated by spikes of black hair.

Even his lips were perfection. Pouty, pink, and made for kissing.

"I'm Logan," I finally choked out.

Marco retrieved a mug and set it in front of me. "Are you headed to the service station today?"

"Tyler is going to pick me up in a few minutes."

Marco smirked at me. "Let me find you a jacket."

I wasn't sure why I needed a jacket until I heard the rumbling of a motorcycle engine pull up outside. I gladly took the black leather coat Marco offered me and headed toward the noise.

Tyler was dressed in black boots, jeans, and a black leather jacket. I couldn't see his face due to the helmet and large reflective sunglasses on his face. He handed me a helmet.

I put it on and threw my leg over the seat and settled behind him.

"Hang on," he said. "The driveway is rough."

I clung to his waist but couldn't help but notice his muscular thighs through his jeans. I put my feet up on the footrests as I checked out his broad back.

I liked the way his shoulders filled out his jacket.

I inhaled.

He smelled good. I'd been awoken by the aroma of cologne in my room this morning. For a grease jockey, he seemed unusual. I could smell an abundance of hair product as well.

He revved the noisy Harley engine.

Tyler was right. The driveway had me gripping tight to him. Once we were on the road to town, I relaxed my hold and enjoyed the ride. The service station was on the outskirts of town. There were two gas pumps out front and what looked to be a convenience storefront. To one side, two repair bays plus a large open bay which I assumed would be for me.

There were four motorcycles I could see.

Tyler pulled into the motorcycle repair space and turned off his engine. I dismounted and pulled off my helmet. I took a step back as who I assumed was Patrick approached us.

Tyler took off his helmet.

Two words. Blond. Gods. My cock didn't care that they were my new employers. Even with his sunglasses on, you could see that Tyler's face was angelic ... but cocky.

He sneered and released a short laugh.

I was staring. Like seeing a feat of nature, I couldn't pull my gaze away.

All that hair product had been put to good use. He'd used it to tame his wavy, dark blond hair into a style reminiscent of greasers of the 1950s.

I turned my attention to Patrick. I added a third word. Blond. *Greek*. God. His features transcended classically gorgeous. He was wearing a plaid shirt unbuttoned right to his navel.

His chest was smooth and tanned. I could see the ridges of his abs. And his eyes—a piercing blue. The wolf was pure sex in a pair of worn jeans and clunky unlaced boots.

"Hey, I'm Patrick."

Shaking his hand made my cock pay attention. "Logan."

"I'm Tyler."

Another handshake from a calloused hand that I imagined touching my body.

I refocused. I needed to be serious. I'd be working with these two wolves. I needed to be professional, and not be imagining a threesome with them.

"Take a look around the shop," Patrick said. "Let me know if you need any other tools. I'll put an order in. Tyler and I don't have much experience with motorcycles. We can manage tune-ups but that's about it. Danny says you do restorations too?"

I swallowed. "Yeah, I do."

Tyler took off his sunglasses. The same piercing blue eyes, surrounded by the same seductive thick fluttering lashes. Maybe they were brothers.

"I had a couple of our regulars looking to restore some bikes. I'll give them a call. Let them know we have someone in Creekside now."

It seemed Patrick was in charge.

"That would be great." I looked at the bikes around the shop. "What's up with these? Do they need some work done on them? I don't mind starting right away."

"These are our personal collection," Tyler said. "And yes, they could do with a once-over from a professional. Once you look around, have at it. We'd appreciate the help."

I clapped my hands together. "Right. Good." I had a starting point. I was itching to get my hands on the beautiful bikes in front of me. I'd start by disassembling the engines and go from there. I headed straight for the tool drawers to see what I had to work with.

Patrick set a pad of paper and a pen on top of the toolbox.

"I'm serious," he said. "Anything you need."

"Thanks."

Hours later, I didn't notice the sun going down. The sound of the bay doors closing was the only indication the day had passed with me immersed in what I was doing.

"Let's go home," Patrick said and clapped his hand on my back.

It was surreal riding in a truck back to the house. I was seated between the two gorgeous wolves I shared a room with. Them close to me in their beds was going to make sleep difficult.

A shower was first on my agenda once we arrived at the house.

To wash the sweat of work off my skin … and take care of *other* things.

Chapter Three | Harlan

I hung up the phone in Carina's office. Patrick from Creekside Service had called to let me know they'd had a wolf walk into their midst who had loads of experience restoring motorcycles.

I had at least two that needed to be rebuilt entirely. I'd been acquiring collector vehicles for a couple of years. Reese had turned me on to it. I was riding the last bike he'd ever buy.

It was yet another thing that had been taken away from Reese with the loss of his hand. We'd had some epic road trips over the years. I hoped he'd someday climb on the back with me.

It was against my instinct to use *Creekside Service* because it was owned by two wolves from the West Creekside pack. I considered their pack as rivals. There was a repair station in Riverton, but that wouldn't have been any better. Despite the rivalry, I preferred supporting a local business.

Patrick and Tyler were amenable enough.

I lifted my keys. Patrick had told me to bring one of my bikes by for *Logan* to look at. I needed help loading one into the back of my pickup truck. Luckily, two of the meatheads in my house were home from work today. I found them in the living room, gaming.

"Can I get a hand, please?"

"You have two. Use those."

They both found this joke hilarious. They were Omegas. I could make them listen to me if I wanted to, but I wasn't into resorting to pack hierarchy to get what I wanted.

"Five minutes of your time. That's all I'm asking for. I'll bring you back some beer."

I was *not* above bribing.

"A full case." Meathead one rose to his feet. Meathead two copied him.

"Fine. Okay. A full case of that watery shit you two like."

"What do you need help with?"

"Loading my Harley cruiser into the back of my truck."

"You selling it?" The two wolves followed me outside and into the carport. I wheeled the bike to the back of my truck and arranged the straps I'd need to secure it.

"No. I'm finally having it restored."

"It's going to be a sweet ride."

"If the new wolf Patrick has is any good. Supposedly he's been at it for twenty years."

They grunted as they lifted the motorbike straight up and into the back of the truck. I leaped in and began tying down the bike. They stayed to help, making sure the straps were tight.

"Thanks." I clapped my hand into one of the wolf's. "Beer is on its way."

"Bring eggs too."

I rolled my eyes. "Okay … eggs too."

I took the driveway slowly, watching the motorbike through the back window with more than a little anxiety. It was a beautiful machine. One I looked forward to riding this summer.

I bumped down onto the main road and drove toward town. Partway there, my gut clenched and churned, and I thought I was going to be sick. I lifted my hand from the steering wheel. Both my palms were sweating. The closer to town I drove, the more uncomfortable I became.

By the time I reached the service station, I had full-body sweats, and my heart was hammering in my ears. I turned off the truck and looked through the bay doors.

Patrick and Tyler were busy working beneath cars up on the lifts. My ears started ringing. I had to rest my forehead on my steering wheel to quell a wave of anxiety.

I knew exactly what was going on when my cock started throbbing.

I threw my door open, not bothering to close it, and walked toward the garage. My body's internal workings dragged me forward. The world around me fell away.

Fated mate!

The clatter of a wrench being dropped on the cement floor rang out.

My vision blurred around the edges, zeroed in, and became hyper-focused on the wolf kneeling on the floor beside a motorbike. Like a bullseye, I walked straight for him.

His lips were stern and tight, and I could hear him dragging ragged breaths in and out of his nose as he watched me. Everything else about him was frozen, like spooked game.

Logan.

He felt the pull too.

Then he did the most unusual thing. He picked up his wrench and started working again. He was aroused but he kept working even when I stood directly beside him.

I placed my hand on his shoulder.

Logan shivered and pulled away.

Was that a rejection? But he'd felt it too. We were fated mates.

"Omega," I said.

He grunted and almost scuffed his knuckles on a bolt. "Not interested."

I looked up. By this time, Patrick and Tyler had wandered into the workspace. Tyler stood, cleaning his hands on a rag, one eyebrow cocked. Patrick crossed his arms.

"Omega," I said again.

Logan rose to his feet. "Not interested, Alpha."

A sharp pain streaked straight through my heart. "What do you mean? We're fated." Logan growled at me, throwing me off. Why was my fated mate denying me?

"I have no interest in mating with you, Alpha."

My brows dipped. I had no experience in mating practices, but I knew this wasn't the way it was supposed to be unfolding. I looked at Patrick for advice. He shrugged.

I took a chance and touched Logan's cheek with the back of my fingers. He flinched but I kept up the attention, maintaining contact with his bristly skin. He leaned into my touch.

My heart had never hammered so hard. One overzealous move and I knew he would flee from me. Logan needed me to be respectful. Take my time with him.

"Okay, Omega. I won't push you."

Logan's gaze flicked over my shoulder. "You have a bike for me to work on?"

I sighed, withdrew my hand, and stepped back. "84 Harley cruiser."

Logan pushed past me and headed for my truck. He climbed into the truck bed and squatted down to take a better look at the bike. "She's been living rough."

"Just picked her up last year. Can you bring her back to life?"

Logan jumped down. "No promises but I'll do my best. I'll get the ramp." And then he jogged off, nonchalantly, like we hadn't just had a fated connection. As an Omega, he should be down on his knees, begging me to mate with him. Instead, he had turned me away.

Patrick made a face like a blowfish, his eyes wide as he approached me.

"Wow ... that was odd," he said.

Tyler nudged me with his elbow and then leaned against my truck. "Maybe he doesn't like the age difference. He's like 20 years older than you."

"It shouldn't matter," I replied. "We're fated."

"Maybe he doesn't think so," Patrick said.

"Are you serious, Pete?" Tyler said. "Didn't you see Logan? He was primally tethered to Harlan in there. I was sure Logan was going to let Harlan kiss him."

Patrick swatted at a fly buzzing around his head. "I don't know. Strange wolf, I guess."

"And seriously strong-willed," I added and then shushed the other two. Logan was walking back toward us, dragging a metal motorcycle ramp behind him.

It took all four of us, but we soon had the bike inside the garage.

"Will you call me with a quote?" I asked Logan.

"I'll give the quote to Patrick. He can call you."

I wandered in closer to Logan. I so badly wanted to touch him again. He was a gorgeous wolf. Cropped dark hair, trimmed stubble, and soft brown eyes. Above his ears, a spattering of grey strands. I wanted to kiss those ears and suck the lobes into my mouth.

"Can I stop in every couple of days and check on your progress?" I asked.

"That would be fine," Patrick answered on Logan's behalf. Logan was caught in my gaze. There was so much pull between us, I wasn't sure how either of us was going to continue playing this game, but I needed to know why he had turned me down before I tried to move forward with him. Walking away was the hardest thing I'd ever done.

But I left him there amongst the motorcycle parts, my fated mate.

I nearly drove past the one-stop shop where I could buy eggs and beer. I tugged my truck into a spot out front. My palms were still sweating. I climbed out of the cab and noticed that Carina's car was parked a few spots down from me. I pulled open the glass and metal door. Little chimes were brushed by the top of the door, tinkling, announcing my arrival.

I spotted Carina halfway down an aisle. I headed straight for her.

She raised her gaze from the packaging of berries she was looking at.

"Harlan, hun ... you look flushed. Are you sick?"

"I met my fated mate," I blurted out.

Her eyebrows rose. "Where?"

"*Creekside Service*. He's their new motorcycle mechanic."

Now her brows furrowed. "Why aren't you with him? You should be mating."

I looked at my hands. They were trembling. "He turned me down."

"He didn't sense the connection?"

I shook my head. "Oh, no, he sensed it. He melted into my touch."

"But he resisted?"

"Told me he didn't want me." I ran my hand through my hair. "Carina ... I don't know what to do. He's already haunting my every thought. My body is on fire. I need him so badly, I feel ill."

"Can you try again?"

"I don't want to push him. I can't risk having him leave Creekside because of me. That would break me." For now, the only thing I had to look forward to were my visits the garage.

He needed to be there. Not running away into the wilderness.

"You'll figure it out."

I nodded. "I'm meant to buy beer and eggs. The cost of bribery to get a little help."

"You're allowed to assert yourself as an Alpha if you need something done."

"I don't like to push wolves around with my role."

Carina patted my cheek. "Someday, you'll lean into it and take your role seriously."

Maybe someday, but for now, I wanted to go home and curl up in my bed—alone. My fated mate and I should have been in bed together already. Swearing, grunting—and mating.

Howling the song of our commitment.

Trying for a pup.

Instead, I was stuffing a basket full of beer and eggs. I grabbed a bottle of gin for myself. Maybe I could convince my friends to go out tonight. I needed to obliterate Logan from my mind for a few hours. Ease the frantic hold he had on my very soul.

I paid and tossed everything into my truck. I needed to head home first to drop off my promised bribes and then I'd drive back into town to gather up my gang of friends.

Tomorrow, I would figure out what I was going to do.

My friends were reliably game for a night out. By the time we were finished, I was throwing up, dizzy, but still plagued with thoughts of Logan. I stumbled into my bedroom and flopped down on my bed, my head spinning. I rolled onto my back and hauled my jeans open.

My cock was almost hard despite the alcohol. I released it from my underwear. I was predictably dripping with precum. I closed my eyes and pictured Logan's face and his trim delectable body. I imagined him naked, waiting on my bed for me.

I spread my precum all over my cockhead with my thumb. I tasted it to ramp my desire and then stroked my cock in steady movements. I kept pumping until I couldn't contain a moan.

I was slowly escalating to a climax.

Tears rolled from my eyes, and I had to stop. I let my hands fall to my sides as I looked up at the ceiling. Encouraging seed from my body without my mate would feel empty.

I pinched the bridge of my nose. I wanted him desperately. We were fated to spend our lives together. I wanted to know everything about him. His past and present, and his future plans.

I sucked in a shuddering breath. I needed to be strong and not push him.

I wasn't convinced I could do it.

I MANAGED TO STAY AWAY from the garage for three days. Not that I didn't drive past it. I did every time I was in town, hoping to catch a glimpse of Logan. Occasionally, I could make him out amongst the motorcycles, looking gorgeous as he toiled with the metal beasts.

Today, I parked my truck out front to check on the progress of my bike. I waved to Patrick as I stepped through the bay doors. I had promised myself; I wouldn't rush to Logan's side.

"Morning," I said to Patrick.

"You're here early."

"I have a job in an hour. Early start."

"I heard you're working for Mark now."

"Not quite. We're partners in the business."

"Nice," Tyler said, emerging from beneath a car.

"My first official job as *Cooper Plumbing* today. It's with one of my long-standing customers. I needed to assure him nothing was going to change."

"Customers will come around in time."

"How's my bike looking?" I asked Patrick.

"Well … it's in pieces at the moment, but he seems to know what he's doing."

I hitched my thumb over my shoulder. "I'm going to take a peek."

I steadied myself and turned toward the far bay. My heart skipped a few beats when I caught sight of him. He was focused on what he was doing. Or that's the illusion he was trying to project. Every few seconds, as I stood there watching him, his gaze would flick up to me.

I crossed the garage until I was standing within a few feet of him.

"How's she looking?"

"Like she's going to take me weeks." Logan looked up at me. You could see the restraint at the point of breaking on his face. His eyes were wrinkled at the corners, his lips taut.

"I got your quote."

"Yes, Patrick told me you approved it."

My fingers twitched at my side and "Can I buy you a coffee?" spilled from my mouth.

Logan's gaze softened. "We have coffee here."

"I'm sure the coffee at *Creekside Delicatessen* is better," Patrick offered.

"He's not wrong there," Tyler piped up.

Logan sighed and smiled at me. "Maybe next time."

His smile almost melted me. I'd cherish it along with the way he had responded to my hand on his face. Logan was like a puzzle, and I was going to let him turn over the pieces at his pace.

"Next time." I smiled back at him.

His breaths shortened and I was sure I heard a muffled whine.

This was going to be agony for both of us.

I PACED MYSELF, only going to check on my bike once a week. I didn't bring up going for coffee again. Slowly, there was an ease developing in our conversations.

I stood beside Logan at a workbench to see what he was doing with my motorbike engine. He explained what parts he had replaced and how they would improve the running of the bike.

Some parts lay on the far end of the workbench. He'd had them re-chromed. They looked shiny and new. He'd ordered a new black leather seat. I was fascinated by his attention to detail.

"I should be able to start putting her back together by the end of the week," Logan said.

"When can we get her on the road?"

"I'll be giving her a test ride on Monday of next week." Logan bit his bottom lip as he looked at me. "You could come by for that. Have a go yourself."

"I would love that. So far, you look like you've done an amazing job."

"She's been a pleasure to work with." Logan wiped his hands on a rag and set it down. His brow furrowed as he looked at it. He turned his attention back to me.

"It's terrible service station coffee but maybe we could have one in the back office."

It felt my spirit soar. My inner wolf was close to howling. I could feel my increasing heartbeat in my throat. Logan had extended an invitation for more. "I'd like that."

Logan moved away from the workbench and motioned for me to follow him. We arrived at the convenience store area of the service station. At the back, two large coffee urns. I took my turn filling a cup and adding a couple of packets of creamer to my coffee.

Patrick made the fingers-crossed sign to me as we passed him in the repair area of the service station. The office was at the back of the bays. Logan lifted a pile of papers off a second chair and rolled it toward me. The back was broken. I needed to make sure I didn't push against it.

"I really appreciate all of the work you've put in," I said.

Logan smiled and lifted his cup in mock toast. "You're paying me."

"Worth every penny. She's going to be gorgeous."

"Any plans for trips?"

"Yeah, I'll probably head east. There's some beautiful scenery out that way."

"Once I have my own bike, I'll check it out."

My fingers tingled as I considered my next sentence.

"You could always come with me."

"Like ride on the back with you?"

"That's typically where passengers go, but I'd let you drive as well."

Logan sighed. "Harlan, I really don't want to do anything with you."

I leaned forward in the chair. "Why? Please help me to understand. We're fated."

Logan tipped his head as looked at me. "I'm not what I seem to be."

I set a serious crease on my forehead, confused. "I don't understand."

Logan's breath turned shallow and quick. "I'm not an Omega."

My eyebrows rose. "But your scent ...."

"Doesn't represent who I am inside."

"You think you're an Alpha?"

"I *am* an Alpha. I can't mate with another Alpha."

I chewed on my bottom lip as I considered what Logan just told me. I had never heard of a wolf identifying differently from what their scent revealed. Logan had the ability to whelp pups.

I wanted to know more.

"When did you know?" I asked.

This time Logan's eyebrows rose. "That doesn't make you want to run?"

"It *makes* me curious."

"Okay." He folded his hands in his lap. "I suppose I've always known. Moreso after I shifted at sixteen. My sire and carrier weren't supportive. My sire used to beat me for it."

I reached for and placed my hand on his knee.

"I'm so sorry that happened to you."

Logan shrugged. "You get used to it."

"No one should ever have to get used to that."

"It is what it is, I suppose. Made me more determined."

I couldn't believe anyone would punish this gentle wolf for being himself. There was a lot of cruelty in the world. Cruelty and ignorance. He wasn't going to get that from me.

I took a chance and gripped his hand. "I see you, Alpha."

Tears pooled in Logan's eyes and ran down his cheeks.

"Thank you, Harlan."

"I'm honored you would share this part of yourself with me, and I promise, as your fated mate, I'm here for you. You can come to me with anything."

Logan sniffed and clung to my hand. "You're not what I expected from someone so young."

"You'll find I grew up a long time ago." I smirked. "Aside from the occasional night out."

Logan's chest rose and fell as he stared at me. He was the first to make a move by cupping my face. He brushed his thumb back and forth over my lips.

"It's brutal trying to resist you," he said and lowered his hand.

My tension was released in an exhalation. "Then why are you resisting?"

"We're two Alphas."

I gripped the back of his neck and brought our foreheads together. "I don't care."

"I don't want to be seen as an Omega."

"I will tell everyone you're my Alpha."

"You say that now."

I pulled back and looked into his anxious brown eyes. "I don't make promises lightly. I promise you that I will never refer to you as my Omega. Not ever."

"I want to believe you."

"Then do." I brought our lips to within a whisper of each other. "I need you, Alpha."

The word, "Okay," dissolved into a moan as our lips met.

Chapter Four | Logan

I felt as if I was floating. I couldn't believe I'd kissed him. I touched my lips. I could still feel him on me. After the kiss, Harlan left me alone to think about everything.

Harlan was right. He was so much more mature than his years. I was sure he was still a teenager. The age difference had been unexpected after I first sensed him.

"I will never refer to you as my Omega. Not ever." Those words of Harlan's had triggered something in me that bordered on trust, but I didn't know him well enough to fully trust him yet.

I finished installing the refurbished metal detail to the fuel tank. It was the finishing touch. It was dusk. A few more minutes of light. Still enough time to take her out for a ride. Except I had promised Harlan I wouldn't be riding her until Monday. I stepped back to look at her.

She was stunning.

"Nice job," Patrick said to me. "And by the sounds of things, she's purring like a noisy kitten."

"It's a beautiful rumble."

"You bike guys and your loud engines." Patrick crossed his arms and shifted his weight to one leg. "So, you and Harlan … anything happening there."

I didn't mind Patrick asking. We'd become close during the weeks we'd been bunking together. He and Tyler had been welcoming in the extreme. I appreciated them.

I rarely imagined them naked anymore.

"We're working through things," I replied.

"You could do worse. For an East Creeksider, Harlan is a decent wolf."

"I'm sensing that. His age is a stumbling block, though. How old is he?"

Patrick shrugged. "I don't know. Nineteen. Twenty. Something like that. Harlan was a kid when he first started coming in here with his brother, Reese."

"You've known him for a long time."

"He was a feisty little kindergartener when I was in grade ten. A terror on the playground. Tyler and I would sit on the bleachers watching him rip around trying to prove himself."

"He's confident. I've sussed that out."

"Why did you turn him down at first?"

"We needed to get some understandings out of the way. I didn't think he'd go for it."

"Cryptic."

"If things progress with Harlan, I'll explain what I mean." I rubbed a bit of chrome with a soft cloth. "You've known Tyler since you were teenagers?"

"His family moved to Creekside when we were thirteen. We moved into Carina's house together five years later and took over the mechanics business from my sire two years after that."

"You seem close."

"Known each other for 17 years. He's my best friend."

"No luck finding a mate?"

Patrick wrinkled his nose. "Tyler and I prefer things the way they are." He pointed to the bike. "Are you going to take her out for a ride?"

"Monday. I promised Harlan he could be here."

Patrick nodded and smirked at me. "You're feeling things, aren't you?"

"I'm warming to him. He's been good about giving me my space."

"I've seen the two of you huddled over here, talking. I hope it works out for you."

"We'll see." I tossed the cloth on the workbench. The bike couldn't get any shinier. I wanted it to be perfect for when Harlan saw it. He was going to be floored.

I couldn't wait to see the look in his eyes.

Patrick was right. I was starting to feel things. Despite his age, Harlan had a wisdom and kindness about him I found appealing. Plus, I found his broody appearance to be a turn-on.

He had the appearance of a quintessential bad boy. Sharp cheekbones and chiseled chin. Dark hair and eyes that you could sink into the depths of. Full kissable lips and a chill demeanor, like nothing fussed him. He was all Alpha and I found it difficult to concentrate around him.

"Where'd you go?" Patrick teased and punched me in the arm.

I smiled. "Thinking about him."

"You want me to phone Lucas? Get you permission to go on East Creekside land?"

The rapid beat of my heart at the suggestion almost convinced me to say *yes,* but I wouldn't know what to say to him if I showed up at his doorstep. I wasn't ready to mate with him.

"No, I'm good. I'll see him on Monday."

"Suit yourself."

Patrick walked around the shop, closing bay doors, and shutting off lights. Tyler had taken one of the bikes home earlier. He was heading out on a ride tomorrow.

After Patrick locked up, we piled into his truck and drove home. The sun had set by the time we arrived. The headlights caught a dark figure sitting on the front steps of the house.

My body reacted, drawing me to him.

I climbed out of the cab and went to him. Patrick dashed past us and into the house.

"Harlan. What are doing here?" I asked.

"I called Carl. Asked for permission to come on your territory. I needed to see you."

"Carl knows?"

"He does now. Told him I needed to see my Alpha. He seemed confused. Did I do something wrong? Was I not supposed to say anything?"

I rubbed my forehead. "He doesn't know I'm an Alpha yet."

Harlan rose to his feet. "I'm so sorry. I thought you would have told your pack leader."

"Not your fault. I should have." I expected my anxiety to rise as a response to the impending conversation with Carl but being with Harlan made me feel calm.

"I thought we could go for a run together," Harlan said.

That sounded like exactly what I needed. Breathe in some fresh air. Work my muscles. I hadn't spent much time in wolf form since I'd arrived in Creekside.

"I'd love that."

Harlan cupped my face and licked his lips. "Can I kiss you again first?"

I moved closer until our chests touched, our bellies colliding with every inhalation. I wrapped my arms around his waist. I liked being this close to him. He was slightly taller than me. He brought his other hand to hold my face. The kiss was soft and full of affection.

The kiss continued—gentle. No tongues. No trying to overpower one another. Just a sharing of intentions. That we were going to see where our connection led without pressure.

We parted, both breathing heavily.

"Let's shift," Harlan said, backed away, and removed his light coat. I was slow to join him. I was focused on him undressing. By the time I was unzipping my jeans, he was nude.

His body was lean, not yet filled out, but he was muscular. The moonlight played on all the little contours and curves. I lowered my gaze. His cock had thickened while we'd been kissing.

I returned my attention to removing my clothes.

Harlan's gaze wandered over me when I'd dispensed with all of them. He must have liked what he saw because he whined, then turned from me, and shifted.

I shifted and we took off for the forest. For a distance, I followed him, and then I took the lead. We were two Alphas running. We would take turns leading the way.

I let the calm of my wolf form wash over me as we chased after each other. This was simple. In this form, all my anxieties were put on hold. This was Harlan and me out in the wilderness.

My fated mate.

Harlan caught up with me, snuffling as he launched himself playfully at me. We ended up in a heap, panting. He whined and nudged my muzzle with his. I growled and placed a loose grip on his muzzle with my teeth. It was an act of affection. As I released him, Harlan leaned against my shoulder, barking and play-snapping at my nose. The banter felt natural and destined.

Any longer and we'd take it too far. I leaped to my feet and looked around to get my bearings. The nights were still chilly. I could smell woodsmoke from the pack compound's fireplaces.

I started trotting back toward home.

When we reached the clearing in front of the houses, we shifted back. I kept from watching him this time, letting him dress without my roving eyes.

I didn't bother with my shoes. Just made my way to the house's landing. Harlan followed me up the steps and stood outside the front door with me.

"That was nice," I said.

"You have a beautiful black sheen to your fur."

"I didn't expect yours to be brindle."

Harlan smiled at me. "Is that a deal breaker?"

"Not for a second." I played with the short hairs above his ear with my fingertips. "You were breathtaking." I sighed as he pulled me into his arms and his mouth found mine.

This time we were both more demanding. Starting tentatively, playing along each other's lips with our tongues, then piercing the warmth to sample the exquisite taste beyond.

We both moaned and grappled with our offending clothing. Before we had a chance to take the lust-filled desperation too far, Harlan softly gripped my wrists to stop me.

"This isn't the right time or place," he said. "I want you to feel cherished. Getting each other off on the front steps of your house doesn't scream romantic."

I closed my eyes. He was right. That's where we'd been heading. Jerking each other off on the porch of Danny's house where any number of wolves might see us.

I'm not sure why. But I started crying.

Harlan brushed some tears from my cheek. "What's wrong?"

"I think I'm scared."

"Do you need me to back off for a while?"

I shook my head. "No, you're being perfect. Maybe that's what's scaring me. When it comes time to mate, I know you'll be a perfect gentleman, letting me decide what happens." I shuddered through a trembling breath. "I thought I knew what that would be but with you it's different."

"You're right. I'll do whatever you're most comfortable with. You're my Alpha. If that means you planting your seed in me every time, then that's what we'll do."

It was time to uncover more of my story. "I've been mated before."

"For how long?"

"As long as it took for my mate to confront me about my inability to put a pup in him."

"Your mate was an Omega?"

"A friend. We decided to give it a go. See if we could defy the odds."

"Logan … it's unlikely you could get an Omega pregnant. You knew that."

"I know, but lots of mated pairs don't have pups." I shrugged. "I thought maybe companionship would be enough for him."

"It wasn't?"

"We fought a lot. I was asked to leave by the leader."

"For fighting?"

"For what I know to be true."

"They didn't acknowledge that you're an Alpha?"

"They called me delusional."

Harlan wrapped his arms around me and held me to him. I cozied into his embrace. I felt warm and protected in his arms. Despite the fact he was slighter than me, he made me feel safe.

His age was becoming less of an issue.

My fated mate was strong and capable.

And caring—so very caring.

"I'm going to go," Harlan said. "You're away from that pack now. I think you'll find that Carl will be understanding. Lucas only has good things to say about him."

"I hope you're right."

I watched Harlan take every step away from me. When his truck was backing down the driveway, I gathered what courage I could and went into the house.

Danny was hovering in the front entry.

"Everything go all right with Harlan?" he asked me.

"Amazing. We went for a run together."

"Romantic."

I smiled. "It was."

"Can I talk to you for a second?" I knew what was coming. Carl had talked to Danny about what Harlan had inferred over the phone. They'd need clarification.

I followed Danny into the back hallway.

"When Harlan called Carl," Danny started. "He said he wanted to see his *Alpha*."

I nodded.

"Explain that to me," Danny said.

"Not much to explain. I'm an Alpha."

"Your scent says otherwise."

I wrapped my arms around my stomach. This might be it. After almost a month, I might find myself out in the wilderness again. A wolf without a pack.

A small spark of warmth filled my belly.

Harlan wouldn't let that happen to me.

"I know I'm able to bear pups. I'm not delusional. And I know my chances of putting a pup in an Omega are slim." I peered into his eyes to see where his acceptance or lack of was landing. "But I'm an Alpha. I've known it my entire life. I can't explain it. I just know."

I nearly crumpled with relief at Danny's next words.

"And you're willing to be with another Alpha?" he asked.

"Yes," I gripped the front of his shirt. "Yes, Harlan is my fated mate."

"Patrick and Tyler say you're doing a good job."

I released his shirt, thrown by the change in direction. "I'm working hard."

"That's what Carl is most concerned about. Your contribution to the pack." Danny jerked his thumb over his shoulder. "We've started plating up some meat in the kitchen."

I trailed behind Danny. Patrick and Tyler were leaning against the kitchen counter, waiting for their turn to feed after the Alphas. Danny clapped his hand on my back.

"Grab a plate, Alpha. You'll be feeding first with us."

I couldn't stop the stream of tears that escaped and coated my cheeks. I was being accepted for who I was … for the second time in my life. The first time was with Harlan.

MONDAY ROLLED AROUND far too slowly. I wasn't sure what time Harlan was planning on coming by. We hadn't talked since Saturday when I'd let some walls fall away.

I never could have imagined myself with another Alpha. It had always been something that I vehemently tried to avoid, but Harlan was different than any other Alpha I had ever met.

He'd invaded my dreams. His lips on mine. His naked body in the moonlight. I'd snuck into the bathroom more than once over the weekend to try to clear my system of him.

Patrick, Tyler, and a few of the other wolves snickered at me each time I emerged, the scent of my spilled seed following me into the hallway.

I went over the tailpipe one more time, polishing it. I wanted Harlan's motorcycle to be everything he dreamed it would be. Finished for the hundredth time, I decided to grab some paperwork from the office. I had a few more motorcycles that had come in for me to work on.

I should have had my senses turned on, but I was thinking about Harlan. I wasn't paying attention. I knew Patrick and Tyler weren't in the garage, but I assumed they were in the parts room.

Wrong.

I flung open the office door to the sight of Tyler on his knees at Patrick's feet, giving him head so good, Patrick had his chin tipped up, eyes closed—swearing quietly.

That all stopped when the door banged against the filing cabinet.

Tyler dropped Patrick's cock like it was a hot pepper.

"I thought you locked the door," he said to Patrick.

"I thought you did."

I spun and took off for my end of the garage. I was pacing in circles, muttering, when Tyler found me. I'd had no idea. I'd been sleeping beside them for a month without a clue.

They must hate me for ruining their sleeping arrangement by invading their room. If they were a mated pair, why hadn't they told me? Was it because they were two Omegas?

"Slow down, Logan," Tyler said. "You're going to wear a circle in the floor."

I came to a stop. "I'm so sorry. I had no idea."

"Not your fault. We should have locked the door."

I shook my head. "No, not that." I swiped my hand through the air. "Okay, that, but also moving into your room, ruining your privacy."

Tyler laughed. "No, you're reading too much into it. Patrick and I don't rut or sleep in the same bed together. Just give each other the occasional blow job."

"You're not mates?"

"With Patrick?" Tyler laughed again. "I have no desire to be mated to another Omega."

I lowered my voice. "Does anyone else know?"

"Worse kept secret ever," Patrick said as he strode toward us. "The whole house knows."

Maybe that's what Carl had meant when he said Patrick and Tyler were a handful. Two Omegas messing around with each other. Sure, it happened ... but not long term.

I was saved from discussing their relationship further when Harlan pulled up in his truck. I jogged to his door to greet him. Instead of the kiss I wanted to give him, I shook his hand.

I was a jumble of confusion.

Harlan's brow furrowed. "You all right? You look like you've seen a ghost."

"I'll tell you next time we're alone."

Harlan smiled at me. "You want to be alone with me again?"

I nudged him. "You know I do." I could feel heat rise in my face. There was something about Harlan's presence that almost made me feel nervous. Nervous and giddy.

"Let's start with this bike first." Harlan looked over my shoulder into the bay. "Oh, my god ... are you serious?" He pushed past me and wandered up to the beauty that was his bike.

He cough-laughed and covered his mouth. When I joined him, he shoved me playfully. "This can't be the same bike. You didn't do this." He stroked the handlebars. "She's gorgeous."

"I'm happy how she ended up."

"Happy? God, Logan, you're a damned wizard." Harlan flung his arms around me and hauled me into a breath-killing embrace. I clung to him, wrapping my arms around his waist.

He kissed my cheek again and again until I was laughing. I'd never had anyone be so exuberant with their appreciation of the work I'd done for them.

Harlan released his grip on my body and placed his hands on my face.

"I need to kiss you," he said.

I smiled and ducked my eyes. "I have no objections."

"Good." He swayed back and forth and ever so slowly brought his lips to mine. So deep—but so gentle, exploring as if we weren't in a public place. His tongue tickled mine, then lapped across my lips. It surged back to search my mouth for fulfillment.

I hummed against his lips as I ran my hands through his thick black hair. It was long enough for me to secure a couple of good handfuls. He moaned as I tightened my grasp.

I felt as if one of the wolves clearing their throat was the only thing that had stopped us from taking this further. If we'd been alone, I might have been encouraging Harlan into the office.

He'd turned my emotions inside out like a sweater that had been unfurled to reveal a multitude of colors you wouldn't have known were there without taking the time to find out.

"Let's take this bike out," Harlan said.

"Moment of truth." I reluctantly stepped away from him and retrieved two helmets. He put his on and threw his leg over the seat. I climbed on behind him, very aware of the fact my hardening cock was pressed to the base of his back. I placed my hands on his hips.

My heart fluttered a little as Harlan started up the bike. Patrick was right. She purred. Harlan turned the wheel and eased us toward the door. Once we were outside, he revved the engine.

It filled the bays with vibrating noise.

"Hang on," Harlan said and took off for the road. He was easy with her for the first mile or so, then he opened her up. My exhilaration gave me shivers. We were flying down the road.

I moved my hands from Harlan's hips to his chest. I clung to him, feeling his breath beneath my fingertips. I shifted closer so my chest was plastered to his back. If I could have climbed inside him, I would have. Harlan slowed and pulled off the main road onto a nearly hidden road.

The surface went from paved to packed dirt. It felt like we drove for another 10 minutes. The road eventually opened into a clearing containing a serene lake.

Harlan stopped and switched off the bike.

"I love this place," he said. "My brother and I used to come here in the summer to swim."

"Not anymore?"

"No, my brother has a family now that keeps him busy."

I removed myself from the bike. Harlan followed and set his helmet on the seat. I did the same. He reached for and took my hand and led me to the water's edge.

It was a beautiful spot. Clear still water surrounded by immense cedars and spruce that were reflected on its surface. A few ducks dodged around; a string of ducklings paddling to keep up.

"There's a nice flat patch of grass over here," Harlan said. "Let's sit."

He was the first to sit. He tugged on my hand until I joined him. My body knew what it wanted. Harlan tipped me back until I was laying on the grass. He hovered above me and used his finger to trace my lips. I gripped the back of his neck and pulled him to me.

"My fated mate," he whispered against my lips.

"My Alpha."

He descended on my mouth with a level of desire I hadn't experienced with him yet. With my hands in his hair to keep him on my lips, Harlan moaned and pressed his chest to mine.

He swept his hand onto my shoulder and shifted his weight until his body was covering mine.

I groaned and closed my eyes, my lust spiraling out of control as his hard cock ground against mine; his thick perfection that yearned for me. I inhaled the scent of his arousal. It was intoxicating—dancing on my senses like I'd been waiting for it my entire life.

Maybe I had been. He was my fated mate.

Harlan grunted as he thrust against me. I met every one of his undulations, deepening the kiss. I wanted to taste all of him. I moved my hands from his hair to his ass, encouraging him.

I whined when he separated from my lips.

"I don't want our first time to be here," he said.

"Where do you have in mind?" I was feeling brave. Probably from the high I was riding from having him on top of me, his hot breath puffing past my lips. His taste still on my tongue.

In my right mind, I was terrified to find myself in bed with Harlan, navigating what we wanted from each other. I was confused as to what I wanted my role to be.

We were two Alphas. Neither of us held mating rights over the other.

"I have my own room," he replied.

Harlan had expressed he would be content being seeded by me. I touched his face. My inner Omega wanted more than to seed *him* and that truly frightened me.

"I'm sorry, Harlan, I'm not ready."

Harlan tucked his lips between his teeth. I couldn't tell what he was thinking. He licked his lips as he stroked the hair above my ear and looked into my eyes. "I would never pressure you."

He looked at my chin. "I just thought this was going somewhere what we were doing."

"It might have … I might have stopped you. I don't honestly know."

His tear-glazed gaze flicked back to my eyes. "But you *do* want me."

I gripped his shoulders. "Oh, Harlan, my Alpha, don't ever question that. I want you. I want what we'll someday share." I'd never wanted a physical connection as much in my life.

"You're just not ready yet."

I nodded. "Give me some time to work out some shit in my head." I wiped some tears from his cheeks. In some ways, he was still so young. So fragile. So unsure.

But he was my Alpha and my feelings for him were growing.

"Can you help me get the motorbike to my house?" He sniffed, rolled away from my body, and rose to his feet. My body had never felt so disconnected. As if a piece was missing.

"I'll drive your truck." I clambered off the grass. "You can give me a ride home after."

"Sounds like a plan." He smiled at me but there was hurt in his eyes.

I needed to remind him. I gathered him in my arms and pressed my lips to his ear. "I want you, Harlan Armstrong. Every piece of you. Please wait for me."

His breath hitched. He was on the verge of tears again, but his words were strong. "Forever, my Alpha. I'll wait for you forever."

Chapter Five | Harlan

The drive back from dropping Logan off in West Creekside was the loneliest I had ever felt. That included Reese moving out and leaving me in that room alone.

This hurt deeper. A soul-level depth of ache. Logan was my fated mate and I wasn't going home to him. I should've been headed into his arms. My Alpha. The wolf who interrupted my thoughts every second of every day. After seeing my bike restored, as well as being completely enamored by his sweet, kind, and shy demeanor, I was intensely proud of my Alpha.

He was gifted in the extreme. He'd taken a tired jumble of worn and rusty parts and turned them into a thing of beauty. I wanted to show him off and let everyone know we were mates.

I wanted him in my home where we could curl up and get to know one another better. Share our secrets. Laugh about silly things. Search the depths of what it meant to be fated.

And I wanted him in my bed where I would take my time with him. Memorize every inch of his skin. Taste it. Inhale the full scent of him. Wrap my legs around his waist and kiss him as he filled me. I was desperate for that intimacy. And for the day we'd claim each other.

I pulled up outside the house and looked at it. This wasn't a home without Logan here. I jumped in response to someone rapping on my window.

It was Reese.

I opened my door and joined him on the driveway.

"That motorbike is epic," he said. "Not even going to ask how much it cost to restore it."

"Might have to pick up a second job but I'm thrilled with the way she turned out."

"And how is the restoration artist?"

I smiled. Reese was right. Logan *was* an artist. I'd been keeping Reese in the loop as a relationship formed between Logan and me, but I hadn't told him everything.

"We went to the lake today during our test drive."

"Our secret spot?"

"I hope you don't mind. I was desperate to take him there. To see the beauty of the place."

"Did he enjoy it?"

I nodded.

"But something's wrong," Reese said.

I furrowed my brow. "Not wrong exactly. Just different than I wish it was."

"How so?"

I leaned against my truck. "He keeps telling me he's not ready to mate."

"You said you were going to give him time."

"But what if he's never ready? What if I lose him?"

"Do you think that's what's happening?"

"No." I didn't. I really didn't. Logan had asked me to wait for him. Why would he say that if he was going to bolt? "Maybe I'm over analyzing."

"You do tend to do that."

I draped my arms across my stomach. "I want to hold him in my arms and fall asleep with him. Wake up and kiss his eyelids until he smiles. Suck on every one of his fingers and toes."

Reese brushed his hand down my cheek. "Little brother … I think you might be in love."

"We barely know each other."

"Sometimes love builds quickly from an initial gut reaction to someone. That's how it was with Mark and me. From the first day, our orbits synced. I felt like I'd known him my entire life."

"That's how I feel about Logan. It's like I've never not known him."

"That feeling ... that goes beyond simply being fated. Being fated means you're drawn to each other for the purpose of mating. The trust and support ... and love usually comes later."

"Mating with Logan isn't the reason I want to be with him. We have an ease and connection I cherish. Dropping in on him while he was working on my bike revealed that to me."

"He's more than a fated mate."

I sighed. "He is. He's become my everything."

"But you don't want to tell him in case he thinks you're pressuring him."

"He's scared. I can see it in his eyes."

Reese crossed his arms. "Tell me if I'm prying ... but why?"

I matched Reese's stance. "Because he's an Alpha."

Reese's eyebrows rose and his eyes widened. "Logan is an Alpha?"

"It's complicated."

"I should say so. Why didn't you tell me?"

I smiled at Reese. "I didn't need one of your lectures?"

"Stop." He shoved me and laughed. "You know I'd never judge." He studied me for a moment. "I've never heard of two Alphas being fated mates before."

"Like I said ... it's complicated."

"Okay." Reese clapped me on the back. "Bit of brotherly advice. Keep treating him with respect. Adhere to his boundaries. And even if you don't tell him, shower him with your love and understanding. And commitment. Make sure he knows, you're right there with and for him."

"Planning on doing all of those things."

"Then my work here is done." He looked over his shoulder. "I better get back. Mark Jr. is cutting a few teeth. Don't want him gnawing my beloved mate to death."

"Thank you, Reese."

Reese took a few steps away. "Get some sleep. A bunch of jobs poured in today while you were off with your Alpha at the lake." Then he was off back to his house.

My Alpha.

I felt warm inside.

The house was too noisy when I walked in. Video games blared. Wolves snarled as a bloody shank was being butchered in the kitchen. And a fight had broken out in the basement.

I went to my room and closed the door.

I groaned when someone tapped on it. "Harlan … you home?"

It was Carina.

I hauled it open, and she handed me the cordless phone. "You have a call." I was expecting it to be a customer. I found a cozy spot to curl up on my bed when I heard Logan's voice.

"I miss you," he said.

I smiled. "You just saw me."

"I miss the way you touch me."

"When I'm kissing you?"

"Yes, but at the lake today, when your body was pressed to mine, I felt stuff stir inside me." I could hear him laugh through the line. "That too … but not that."

"I think I know what you mean."

"I really like you, Harlan."

I love you.

"Eh, you're growing on me, I guess."

Logan laughed.

"Could we go for another ride this weekend? You said east of here is nice."

"That's a two-day round trip."

Silence.

"I'd be all right with that," Logan responded at last.

I sat straighter on the bed. I wasn't going to make any assumptions. "We could sleep in wolf form, or we could bring a tent. I have some saddlebags that'll fit the motorbike."

"Bring the tent."

My heart thudded in my chest. Sleeping bags. "Do you mind wearing a backpack with the sleeping bags in it?" Sleeping bags. Plural.

"I think that would be best."

Which thing? Wearing a backpack or having two sleeping bags.

"We'll hunt for game," I said.

"I'd like that … hunting with you."

"I'll pick you up at 7 on Saturday morning."

"I can take the day off work. I'll be ready."

"Have you ever been camping before?" I asked.

Logan laughed. "Once when I was a young pup. Before things got weird between me and my sire. He taught me how to fish."

"I haven't had fish in a while."

"You like it?"

"My brother and I used to catch trout in the lake I took you to."

"We'll have to go back there again."

"I'd like that."

I stretched out on my bed, jamming a pillow behind my head. I spent the next hour like that. There was a lightness in

Logan that hadn't been there before. He opened up to me about his life. His dad. His mate. Their futile attempts to have a pup. His misspent teenage years.

I could relate. I still had my moments now that Reese wasn't there to reel me in. I told him about Reese. How he'd lost his fated mate and his hand, but how he had found a beautiful love.

The last twenty minutes, we'd been in a stretch of banter that left us both in tears of laughter. Logan had a unique take on his life events. Some things shouldn't have been funny; especially to do with his sire, but some of the scenarios he'd found himself in with him were laughable.

I was glad he seemed to have moved past the trauma.

We could have talked longer but Carina knocked on the door, wanting the phone back. It made me jealous of those with cell phones. We could've talked the night away.

And fallen asleep to the sound of each other breathing.

THE WEEKEND FINALLY rolled around. It had been the longest week of my entire life. At 7 in the morning on Saturday, I parked outside Logan's house.

I did not need to go to the door. He was sitting waiting for me on the steps. I had to take a moment to simply look at him as he approached me. My fated mate was stunning.

He'd donned a black leather jacket over his white t-shirt. I was glad when he zipped it up. It was late spring, but it was still cool in the morning. Plus, I wanted him to be safe.

I sloughed off the backpack I'd stuffed with the sleeping bags and handed it to him. It wasn't too heavy. Logan's broad shoulders would have no trouble with it.

I unlatched and handed Logan a helmet.

"You ready?" I asked him as he swung his leg over the bike and settled himself. I smiled as he wrapped his arms around my waist and tugged me to him. I was going to take that as a *yes*.

Two hours out, the air started to warm.

Three hours later and we were at the first of the scenic spots I wanted to take him to. It was a short hike into the forest. An hour at most. Partway up a riverbed, a spectacular waterfall cascaded tons of water onto the rocks at its feet. Logan gripped my arm in awe as he watched it.

The whole drive was scenic. I pointed out different jutting mountainsides and lakes. We stopped at the side of the road to watch a moose cow and her twin calves feed amongst the reeds of an area filled with birds, and then drove through a grove of cedars that were over 800 years old.

Dusk had long descended when I pulled onto an old logging road. We bumped along slowly until we reached an area I had camped at before. It was flat and there was a creek nearby.

Most importantly, it wasn't part of any pack territory.

We worked quietly to set up camp, enjoying the sounds of the forest around us. While Logan put the sleeping bags in the tent, I collected more wood for our growing fire.

I waited until he sat on the ground in front of the flames, then wedged myself between his legs and leaned back against his chest. He encircled my shoulders with his arms, hands on my biceps, and kissed the back of my head. It was all could do not to howl with contentment.

"Hunt in the morning," Logan said.

"Yeah, I'm good for the night."

Logan tapped my cheek. "Look up."

I leaned my head back on his shoulder and stared up at the sky. The stars were putting on a show. Clear and twinkling. He kissed my cheek and brushed his lips across it.

"I really, really like you, Harlan."

Words stuck in my throat. I wanted to tell him I'd fallen in love with him, but it was too soon. My heart knew what it wanted but I refused to push him. I'd made Logan a promise.

"I like you too, Logan." I laughed. "A lot."

"Should we put this fire out? Go to bed?"

"Yeah, my body is tired from driving all that way."

"I'll drive back."

I reached over my head for Logan's and set my hand on top of his head. "Perfect." We parted and I took on the task of putting out the fire and dowsing it with water to make sure it was out.

Logan was in the tent when I finished. He had a small battery powered lantern I had brought with us illuminating the space. What I saw in the tent gave me conflicting signals.

My mate had zipped the two sleeping bags together to create one large bag. But he appeared to have all his clothes on. I removed my coat, kicked off my shoes, and joined him in the large bag. "It's cold," he said as I laid down beside him.

"It is."

Logan rolled toward me and placed his head on my shoulder, his hand on my belly. I moved my arm until I could hold him against me. He played with my t-shirt as neither of us took a full breath. Like we didn't want to disturb each other.

Or give away what we were both likely feeling.

My cock was so hard. I closed my eyes as Logan rolled tighter to me. I wasn't sure if it was intentional, but his hardened cock pressed against my thigh. Then he rolled back a little.

"Sorry," he said.

"No. No worries."

"I'll turn the lantern out."

"Yup." I nodded my head and swallowed hard. He stretched away from me, and the tent went dark, then he was back. I kissed his head. "So ... I guess we'll sleep."

Logan lifted his head. "Do you mind if I stay here?"

"No. I like it. You're nice and warm."

A long silence stretched between us.

"Were you expecting something to happen?" Logan asked once we were good and uncomfortable with the silence.

"I didn't want to assume anything. Hence two sleeping bags."

Logan laughed. "Blew that one out of the water."

"You surprised me by zipping them together."

"I've been dreaming about falling asleep in your arms."

I kissed his head again—a long firm one. "Me too ... every night."

Again, the silence.

"I want us to get there, Harlan. I really do."

I pinched the bridge of my nose as an urge overtook me. "Can I tell you a secret?"

"Of course. We're fated."

"Mmhm." I needed to tell him. False bill of goods and all that. I didn't want to get to that place with him where we'd mate, and he came away disappointed.

"Harlan, what?" He rose on one elbow.

Just say it.

"I've never mated or rutted before."

"Oh." A single word and then more of that dreaded silence. He settled back on my shoulder and stroked a slow line up and down my chest. "Like ever?"

"You're the first wolf I've ever kissed even."

I could feel Logan smile against my shoulder. "You're certainly good at it."

That made me feel a little better. So far, I'd been running off instinct. Maybe it would be the same with mating. Maybe now that Logan knew, he'd guide me.

"I never thought my fated mate would be a virgin."

I smiled. "Don't you dare laugh at me."

Logan cuddled closer to me. "Wouldn't dare. You mean too much to me."

"I can feel you smiling against my shirt."

Logan snorted. "Okay, I might tease you a little."

I rolled until Logan was beneath me and he squealed with laughter. "Then I'll have to shut you up. I've heard I'm good at kissing. Should I kiss you until you're silent, Alpha?"

He sighed and stroked my face. "Please, my Alpha."

Even in the darkness, I found his mouth because his abrupt exhalations were hot on my lips. I caressed his with mine and clung to his gentle hand on my chest. Then we changed positions; Logan on top of me. His hand sought its way under my shirt, across my belly, and up my chest.

I moaned and grasped his ass as Logan pinched one of my nipples between his fingers, slowly increasing the pressure. My cock throbbed beneath my jeans, wishing those fingers of Logan's were further south. I gasped and laughed as Logan climbed fully on top of me.

He was going to be the death of me.

Our lips' contact broken; Logan dragged his teeth along my jawline. My canines descended as he nibbled the side of my neck—licked and sucked—hard and marked me as his.

He tucked his mouth behind my ear, just breathing my scent in, his cock firm against my thigh. He appeared to make a decision because he moved quickly. His mouth's next target was the center of my chest. Then beneath the sleeping bag and down along my abs.

The top of my jeans.

I saw a whole new set of stars as his hot mouth cupped my cock through my pants. He gnawed and licked, growling. The material was becoming damp from both sides, my precum dampening my underwear. His fingers worked my jeans open and with a sharp tug, they were off my hips.

I coughed in surprise. When my mate decided he wanted to proceed, he didn't do it by half measures. My cock strained against the material of my underwear that hadn't come down with my jeans. Logan ran his lips up and down my shaft, and then licked and nuzzled it.

A low rumbling growl drifted up from beneath the sleeping bag as Logan released my cock from its confines. I swore and jammed my hips up as he gripped my cock and circled my thick cap with his tongue. My body lit up when he used his lips and tongue to clear my slit of precum.

A few pumps within his fist and he descended fully on my cock. His mouth was soft and hot and his tongue busy. A small howl of elation left my lips, then I settled into whining and swearing.

This was so much better than my hand.

He released my cock from his hand and moved both hands until he gripped my ass. He kept up his steady rhythm, my cock sliding in and out of his mouth.

I wanted to touch him. I reached beneath the sleeping bag, ran my hand through his hair, and clung to it. He groaned around my cock and increased his pace. My body felt electrified, all my hairs standing on end. My balls pulled up and the base of my cock became uncomfortable.

Logan pulled off my cock and went back to pumping it within his hand.

"You're knotting," he said.

I ran my free hand through my hair. I'd never knotted before. It burned slightly as my skin stretched. I swore under my breath as Logan sucked my swelling flesh into his mouth.

He dragged his tongue across my sensitive skin, his chest rumbling, then he sucked my cock back into his mouth. Slow then fast, driving me to heights I'd never reached before.

It was almost like a cramp releasing when my knot relented. I threw my head back, thrust my hips up, jamming my cock down Logan's throat, and roared as my seed erupted in an unprecedented spilling. It had been as if I had been coerced into releasing my soul. Logan had done that for me. I kept my hand on his head, rocking my hips as my body slowed.

He dropped my sloppy cock from his mouth and covered it with my underwear. I moved my hand from Logan's head to his arm, encouraging him to rejoin me topside of the sleeping bag.

He squirmed his way up my body, hovered above me, and kissed me.

I could taste myself on him.

An urge overtook me. I gripped the back of his neck and deepened the kiss, sweeping my tongue through his mouth. Logan growled and tangled with my tongue, sharing my seed.

My fervor began to diminish, and the kiss turned more languid. Two wolves reconnecting after an incredible experience. One I hadn't been expecting.

I rolled Logan onto his back, keeping pressure on his lips. I cruised down his body with my hand, enjoying the little moans of enjoyment coming from him.

I reached the front of his jeans. His cock was hard and straining, jutting off at an angle away from its base. I rubbed the heel of my hand up and down it.

Logan broke from our kiss.

"No pressure," he said. "Maybe just stroke it."

"Not a chance." I wanted to feel him in my mouth—taste him on my tongue. Bury myself in his very essence. Inhale every molecule of his scent.

Logan undid his pants, lifted his ass, and slid everything off. I gave him a parting kiss on his lips, then lay a slow row of them from his chin down to the root of his cock.

I'm sure my technique was off, but Logan was soon writhing beneath me. His hands jammed into my hair, his hips bucked … and he filled my throat with his glorious seed.

I was delirious as I joined him in a song of commitment.

Chapter Six | Logan

I smiled, waking with the sweetest sensation. Harlan was covering my face in the most delicate kisses. He'd arrived at my eyelids. I squirmed and reached out for him until he placed his head on my chest. He stroked my forearm with his fingers, his hair tickling my lips.

What we had shared last night had felt unprecedented. I'd mated dozens of times in my life. None of those compared to connecting with my fated mate.

I'd heard that intimate moments with your fated mate took on a transcendent level of desire and fulfillment. I hadn't been prepared for what that would feel like.

Actually mating with Harlan threatened to make my heart stop.

"Should we hunt?" I asked. "Maybe chase down some rabbits."

I smiled when Harlan's stomach growled. "I'll take that as a *yes*," I said.

"In a minute, Alpha. Hold me for a while longer first."

"With pleasure." I hugged him closer to me. He threw his leg over my thighs and kissed my jaw. I tented my fingers and felt my rough stubble. It had always grown fast.

Harlan's face was typically free of any bristles.

He was so young.

"I enjoyed last night," I said.

Harlan shimmied closer. "Me too."

"No longer a virgin," I teased.

Harlan laughed. "I don't feel any different."

"I do. What we experienced together was like nothing I've ever felt before."

"Because we're fated?"

"Mmhm." I closed my eyes and enjoyed the feeling of Harlan's fingers brushing up and down my arm. The tent was heating up. It must be late morning. "We should go. By the time we feed and pack up, it'll be noon. I don't want to get in too late. I have a busy day tomorrow."

"Another bike?"

"A Yamaha MT-09."

"Nice. I have one of those. It was Reese's."

"I guess he can't ride anymore."

"No, but I keep hoping he'll have time to jump on the back and go for a ride with me."

"Might be painful for him."

"Maybe." Harlan shifted and rolled, freeing himself from the sleeping bag. His jeans were still open, the line of his cock visible through his underwear. He tucked himself and zipped up.

If I closed my eyes, I could still taste him on me.

I hummed then joined Harlan in packing up the interior of the tent. We had to separate the sleeping bags to fit them back in their bags. I felt sadness as we stored away what had been our nest. Where we had held each other and shared our bodies. And kissed until our lips were sore.

Undressing to shift felt different this time. I wanted to go to him, have him hold me against him, and engage in a dance that would only end one way. I wanted to caress his insides with my cock and fill him with my seed. It would fall on dead soil, but it would be lovingly planted.

That word *love* had been bouncing around in my head. Moreso since last night. Harlan was so much more than what he appeared to be. On the outside, it was obvious he was a teenager, but on the inside, he was wise beyond his years. On the outside, he was confident. On the inside, he was still unsure of himself. That insecurity would fall away as he aged.

He had the makings of a formidable Alpha. I knew that because from the first moment we met, he had treated me with respect. The foundation for a pack leader.

When I told him I was an Alpha, he had accepted it. My identity hadn't swayed him from wanting me. Every time he called me Alpha, it made my heart sing.

Now, we'd shared our bodies, exposing the most intimate parts of ourselves.

Shifted to wolf form, Harlan and I took off into the forest. We soon caught the scent of a warren of rabbits. Harlan dug into the soil, making them scatter. We were quick to snap up two.

We placed ourselves side by side as we fed as two Alphas.

When we were redressing, everything I'd been mulling over struck me and I teared up. Harlan rushed to my side. "What's wrong? Are you regretting what we did?"

I shook my head. "No." I pulled him into my arms. "You're so incredible."

Harlan held me tighter. "So are you, Logan."

I tucked my face beneath his hair and against his neck and inhaled. He was my perfect mate.

"I think I might love you," I whispered.

There was silence. I could count my heartbeats. There were far too many.

Harlan kissed my ear. "I love you too."

THE ENTIRE TRIP BACK, Harlan clung to me, his thighs tight against mine as I drove. We didn't stop this time. We needed to get home. Words of love had been spoken.

I could no longer resist him.

Occasionally, Harlan's hands would drift up and down my thighs. My cock was so hard, it was difficult to concentrate on the road. I readjusted my focus.

I needed to get us home safely.

Seven hours later, I pulled up outside Harlan's house. My house wasn't suitable for what we had in mind. I shared a room with Patrick and Tyler. Harlan had his own room.

Harlan dismounted and looked up at the house. Even from outside, I could hear the sounds of a warfare shooting game and the loud derogatory exclamations that went along with it.

He turned his head and looked at me.

"I don't want *that* as a backdrop," he said.

"We can't go to my room."

He climbed onto the bike behind me. "Head into town. There's a boarding house. The owner is a Beta from my pack. If she has a room, she'll let us have it."

I felt like a teenager looking for a place to rut away from my protectors, but I agreed with Harlan. I wanted to be able to hear his breath and the beat of his heart. Not gunfire.

Once we arrived in town, Harlan directed to me a quaint-looking house in the middle of the main drag. It looked peaceful and welcoming. I parked out front.

We let ourselves in, hand in hand. A matronly female wolf ambled down the hall toward us from what looked like a kitchen. It was a tight front entry. Just enough room for a coat rack.

Harlan smiled at the wolf. "Mama."

"Harlan, darling." She patted his cheek. "What brings you through my door? Are you sick of living at Carina's?" As she spoke, she eyed me up and down. "I don't blame you."

"Mama, this is my fated mate, Logan." He lifted our clasped hands and kissed my knuckles. "We're looking for somewhere quieter to spend some time together."

"You know I don't rent by the night, Harlan."

"I know. I can pay for a month. Do you have an empty room?"

"I have two. One with its own ensuite."

Harlan smiled at me. "We'd like that one. I need to have a shower."

The implication made my cock throb. An image of Harlan beneath a flow of water careened through my mind. I almost moaned. The scent of my arousal was overpowering.

"I don't usually rent to couples."

"Mama, please." Harlan released my hand and gripped both the grey-haired wolf's. "We haven't had our initial mating period yet. We can't do that at Carina's."

She sighed. "No howling. I don't want you disturbing the other tenants. One complaint and you're out the door. And I want the entire month up front."

I thought Harlan was going to kiss her. Instead, he broke out the most brilliant smile. "Thank you, Mama." He turned to me. "Go up to the room. I need to see about squeezing some money out of my bank account via the bank machine down the road."

I felt bad not being able to cover some of the cost of the room. I'd only been working for just over a month. I didn't have much saved up yet.

Harlan bounced out the front door and I smiled at *Mama*. "Thank you for doing this."

"Harlan is a favorite." She led me up the stairs to the upper floor. There were four doors opening onto the landing. Each one had a number. She led me to number 4, opened the door, and handed me the key. "Lucas hasn't met you yet."

"No, he hasn't."

"Are you past breeding age? Harlan deserves to have pups if he wants them."

Mama being a Beta would have questions. I needed to be entirely honest if I was to become part of Harlan's pack. I fiddled with the key in my hand. It was a discussion that needed to happen. Who's pack we were going to settle with? "I haven't had a heat in over a year."

Mama grunted. "And you're sure you're fated?"

"Yes, and we're in love."

Mama looked off into the distance, then back at me. "Lucas says Harlan has been pursuing you for weeks. Am I to understand you haven't mated yet?"

I exhaled. This Beta was digging hard. "No, we haven't."

She crossed her arms. "I hate to see Harlan without pups."

"That's something we need to discuss … in private."

"Fine." She waved me into the room. "Remember no howling … and no blood on the sheets."

"Noted."

Mama left me in the room. I closed the door and placed my forehead on it as my heartbeat thrummed in my ears. Maybe I *was* too old for Harlan. Maybe he'd be better off finding a chosen Omega mate who could whelp him pups. I crossed the room and sat on the end of the bed.

Not once had he mentioned wanting pups.

Maybe because he knew I couldn't give him any. I'd spoken the truth to Mama. I hadn't had a heat in over a year. I was past my breeding age. But that was Omega thinking.

And I was an Alpha.

The door creaked open and the wolf I had fallen in love with poked his head in. "Oh, good. Right room." He closed and locked the door behind him. "I hope Mama didn't grill you too hard."

"She was very direct."

Harlan wandered over to me and cupped my face in both hands. "What others think about us doesn't even register with me." He brushed his thumb over my lips. "I love you."

I smiled at him, making him grin. "I love you too."

Towering over me as I sat on the bed, my Omega wanted to bow to Harlan. I caressed his hips instead and kissed his abs. Not satisfied, I hooked my fingers beneath his shirt and lifted it slightly until his midriff was exposed. I kissed his belly button and then swirled my tongue in it.

Harlan sucked in a breath and jumped, his belly pulling away from me. I set a kiss at the top of the trail of hair that extended from his muscular abs to the top of his pants.

I licked the entire trail from bottom to top. Again, Harlan jumped and hissed. I wasn't finished with this area of his beautiful body. I shimmied his pants off his hips slightly. Far enough down to expose his hip bones. I wanted to eat them they were so perfect.

I licked and sucked on the protrusions until Harlan jammed his hands into my hair, trembling. I dragged my hands down his thighs to his knees, then back up again. The upstroke shifted to the inside of his thighs. I cupped the front of his pants in one hand.

The thick firm cock I'd had in my mouth last night was too long to fit in my palm. It had been a challenge. I used the heel of my hand to push up on his balls, making him moan.

"Alpha," Harlan whispered.

He wasn't looking for an answer.

I took my time undoing the button on his jeans. The zipper, dragging it down at an agonizingly slow pace. I peeled open his jeans, pulled down on the waistband of his underwear, and licked more of his trail of hair. I put the waistband between my teeth and pulled it away from Harlan's body until I knew the room's air was circulating around his aching cock.

He groaned when I released the waistband, letting it snap back in place. I caressed his cock through his underpants, rose to my feet, and abandoned it to focus on his shirt.

I started with his leather jacket, discarding it on the floor.

I removed his t-shirt by placing my hands on his sides under the shirt and sweeping across his skin from his waist to his ribs, to his underarms, and off over his head.

I kept his arms over his head, letting his elbows rest on my arm. I was able to angle in and inhale the scent under one arm. It was intoxicating. I wound my tongue through the dark coarse hairs until Harlan squirmed and sighed. I kissed the underside of his bicep, then released him.

He had responded favorably when I'd pinched his nipple last night. I brushed my thumbs over them, softly, circling them until they were hard nubs. I gathered them in my fingers and squeezed.

Harlan swore under his breath and draped his arms over his head. He breathed into the slight amount of pain I had introduced him to. I gripped tighter and he coughed out an exhalation.

"Yes," he whispered.

"My beautiful Alpha." I released his nipples and kissed the center of his chest. I sat back on the bed, did away with my coat, and stripped off my shirt. Harlan's lips were parted slightly, and he was breathing heavier than he had been minutes before. I hauled his pants lower.

He adjusted his stance to keep from being pulled off balance.

His pants were off his hips, but his cock was still trapped beneath them, only his glistening cockhead peeking up from behind the waistband of his underwear. I leaned forward and sucked the tip, gathering the taste of his precum in my mouth. It was briny and pure decadence.

Harlan hissed as I continued my exploration of his cockhead. Sucking it in and out of my mouth and swirling my tongue around the thick ridge. Giving him a bit of a reprieve, I pulled his underwear down and trapped the waistband behind his full balls. The placement of the taut elastic material made his balls protrude. I pressed his fiercely hard cock against his stomach and sucked one pink furry ball into my mouth. It was firm, salty, and warm beneath my tongue.

I played with it until it was wet and slick. I pulled down with my lips and released it with a quiet popping sound. Harlan groaned and placed his hands on my shoulders. I moved to the other ball, this time dragging out the amount of time I spent on it. His cockhead was weeping heavily.

I played with his precum with my finger, capping the slit. I released his ball and rose to my feet. I smeared Harlan's lips with his precum. "Open."

He obeyed without a moment's pause. I ran my finger behind his bottom teeth and around his tongue. He clamped his lips on my finger and sucked on it, his tongue playing with the invasion.

I removed my finger, cupped his face, and kissed him. He leaped at the chance to reconnect, his mouth exploring mine with urgency. I turned him as we kissed until the back of his thighs were against the bed. One tiny push with my fingers on his chest and he sat down.

I kept pushing until he was lying down, his broody eyes staring up at me. His thick lashes fluttered, and he licked his lips. I squatted, untied his boots, and removed them, then gripped his jeans and pulled everything off. His pants and underwear landed in a heap next to his boots, shirt, and jacket.

Next were his socks. Once I had him naked, I took a moment to admire him.

This was my Alpha. My fated mate.

I caressed his legs with both hands from knees to thighs and shifted to kneeling. I wanted to taste every piece of him, starting with his cock. I pulled his foreskin tight to his body. His cockhead was tight and crimson, a bead at his slit, and it slid along my tongue with ease. This time I was ready for the length and girth of it. I swallowed around it, making Harlan squirm and swear.

His hands moved from gripping the bedding to grasping my hair. He pumped his hips up and down, filling my mouth as he held my head in place. My Alpha was learning.

I slurped and released him. "Flip over. Get yourself up the bed."

When Harlan rolled over, I had to take a second. His ass was round and firm. Two amazing handfuls. I removed the rest of my clothes as he positioned himself.

The bed dipped and creaked as I climbed on. I straddled his legs down by his knees, my ass resting on his calves. I cupped his ass with both hands and massaged them, pulling his cheeks apart so I could see his hole. It was perfect, tight, and pink. Waiting for me.

I eased off and brushed one hand back and forth over one globe of his ass. I raised my hand and gave him a quick smack on the rear. His flesh jumped and he groaned the word, "Yes."

I smacked the other cheek. He raised his hips and then drove his cock into the bedding. This was turning him on. My Alpha was going to be fun to play with.

I lay down a series of smacks, back and forth between his two globes until they started to pink up. I moved on, placed my thumbs at the peak of his thighs, and peeled him open. I ran my thumb across his hole. It jumped and pinched closed tighter.

"Please," Harlan cried.

I shifted and encouraged Harlan to open his legs. I settled between them laying on my belly. I stroked his thigh to relax him. His ass unclenched, soft, and I gently pried apart his cheeks until I could see my target. I licked my finger and circled his hole. It jumped, pulsing.

"Alpha," he whined.

I held him open, moved forward, and ran my tongue over the tight pucker.

Harlan swore and pulled away from me. I grabbed him around the hips and hauled him back. I waited for him to submit and calm himself. He gathered a pillow to cling to.

"Okay," he whispered.

I pulled him open to expose him and made another attempt with my tongue. This time, he didn't propel himself away from me. I immersed myself in his musky scent as I licked and prodded his hole. I flicked my tongue back and forth across it, then pierced my way inside.

I pulled back. I needed a better angle.

"I need you to roll over," I said as I moved out from between his legs.

Harlan did a quick spin. He had some idea of what I was doing because he hitched his legs up, using his hands to keep his legs raised and open. I ran my finger across his wet hole, then sank inside him. The sound he emitted was orgasmic. And he was as slick as an Alpha could get.

I repositioned myself, clasped his ass in both hands and began a new assault on his hole, this time with more fervor, licking and sucking. Teasing and prodding. Every time he groaned; my cock throbbed. I reached through his legs and pumped his weeping cock.

I ran my tongue across his hole and onto his balls, wetting them. I went from his balls to his cock, sucking it into my mouth. I worked it until Harlan started thrusting his hips.

I dragged my tongue down his cock, across his balls, and back to his hole, tickling it. I slipped a finger back inside. He was loose enough for a second—then a third, pumping.

I used the pads of my fingers to tap and caress his prostate.

"Alpha, please," Harlan whimpered. "Mate with me."

I rose on my knees and surged forward, putting my hands on either side of his chest. I leaned down and kissed him. He grabbed my head and lost all restraint, devouring my mouth.

I pulled away and looked down at him. His pupils were blown wide, his beautiful pale blue color barely visible. He was panting and licking his crimson lips.

He was beautiful.

I took my cock in one hand, balanced myself on my elbow, bent a knee, and slipped into the warmth that was Harlan's body. I grunted and thrust higher. Harlan took my entire length with a sigh. He brushed his hands through my hair and smiled at me as if he was welcoming me home.

I withdrew and pushed into him.

He groaned and clung to my shoulders; his legs still splayed. I layered myself on him, making sure I could still reach his mouth as I pumped into him. He lowered his legs and wrapped them around my waist, pressing his heels to my ass to encourage me, pulling me closer each time my hips met the back of his thighs. Harlan tipped his head back and bit his bottom lip, moaning.

"More," he whispered.

My cock jerked, ready to increase my pace. I doubled my speed and ferocity, bashing against his ass; the sound filling the room. Harlan's moans turned to growls.

The change in his voice meant he was getting close. I changed my position so I could watch his cock. He didn't move his hands to grip it. Kept them on my shoulders.

A quiet howl escaped his lips and his cock pulsed, spilling seed all over his belly until it was painted, and his slit was drooling. I needed to capture his mouth.

Once I had control of his lips with mine, my thrusts became more urgent. I felt the coil in my gut start to unwind. I released shuddering breaths into Harlan's mouth as I seeded him.

I needed to continue the intimate contact. I pumped in and out of him, slowing my pace until I couldn't support myself any longer, I was so spent. I lay down on Harlan's chest and he ran his fingers through my hair. We basked in the silence for a while.

"That was more than I expected it to be," Harlan said.

"It felt like coming home after wandering in the wilderness my entire life."

I closed my eyes and enjoyed the feel of Harlan's chest rising and falling.

"It did, didn't it," Harlan replied. "I've never felt so whole and complete."

I smiled. "And we managed to not howl. We need our own place."

"I'll talk to Lucas. Lucas' brother Bryant and his family are moving out of their cabin soon. The pack built them a house to accommodate their growing brood."

I lifted my head. "You want me to join your pack."

"Yes ... I mean ... we'd need to talk about it first."

I rolled away and lay beside him. "My pack is new to me, but they've been good to me."

"I've been with my pack my entire life. And I'm in business with Reese's mate."

"I'm working with Patrick and Tyler."

Harlan sighed. "It would be unusual, but you could keep working for them."

I laughed. "That reminds me. I walked in on them the other day."

"Mating?"

"No, Tyler was on his knees giving Patrick a blowjob."

"Mm. Picturing that makes me happy." Harlan laughed. "They're both so hot."

I nudged Harlan's shoulder. "You're mated now."

Harlan turned his head and smiled at me. "Mated and in love."

I stroked his face. Every molecule of me loved him. Now we knew, we were compatible in and out of bed. He'd responded so well to me. Been hungry for everything I was doing.

I wanted to be wherever he was.

"I'll join your pack," I said at last. "I'll talk to Patrick and Tyler." Harlan grinned and kissed me. I'd never get tired of his lips on mine. I turned to face him. "Shower?"

I waggled my eyebrows at him.

"So soon?"

I laughed. "You'll find I have the stamina of a stallion."

"My Alpha is going to make me very happy."

I reached over him and pinched his ass. "Starting now."

Harlan squealed as he leaped off the bed and ran to the ensuite bathroom.

Chapter Seven | Harlan

We took the full 10 days we were allowed as a new mating pair. Mark had grumbled, knowing our seeding wasn't going to produce any pups. He had more jobs than he could handle. My customer base had come through, trusting my new company with their plumbing jobs.

Patrick and Tyler had told the human owner of the Yamaha motorcycle that Logan was sick and would be back soon to begin the restoration work.

I nuzzled closer to Logan. This was the last morning of our breeding honeymoon. Logan had seeded me so many times that I couldn't make it to the bathroom without needing a hot cloth to clean the inside of my legs. It was a shame my anatomy didn't allow me to carry pups.

I traced my finger down his bare chest.

"You and your mate tried for pups," I said.

"He wanted them."

"And you didn't?"

Logan shifted and squirmed slightly. "I did. I've always wanted pups."

"Do you want pups with me?" Maybe Logan had wanted pups with his last mate because his mate was an Omega. Maybe he viewed our relationship differently.

He rolled to face me. "I would love pups with you. But I can't."

"Because you're an Alpha."

His gentle eyes gazed into mine. "I'm not having heats anymore."

That was definitive. Logan was almost 40. Twenty years older than me. If we wanted pups, we'd need to figure something else out. The humans had a method we could investigate.

"What about surrogacy?"

Logan pulled back from me a little. "You'd mate with an Omega?"

I wasn't sure how it worked but I was sure I didn't have to do that. "No, Alpha. I don't ever want to mate with anyone but you. The humans have a procedure for doing it."

"A random Omega would carry our pup?"

"Doesn't have to be random."

Logan sighed. "Can I think about it some more?"

"Of course." I held his face and kissed him. I wanted to start a family with Logan. He would make an incredible sire. "One final shower before we move into the cabin?"

He smirked at me. "I'm looking forward to having baths with you."

I touched his lips with my finger. "I'm looking forward to claiming you." The no-howling rule had stopped us from performing the ceremony. Howling was an important part of it.

Logan growled and rolled on top of me. "I want to make you mine."

"And you mine. Another week and the cabin is ours."

"Argh." Logan rolled back off me. "I feel like I'm going to burst."

I smirked at him. "I can help you with that … in the shower."

THE WEEK SHOULD HAVE gone by faster. I was busy. Mark was right. We had been inundated with plumbing jobs. I was working from early in the morning until late at night.

Logan and I hadn't seen each other in days.

Bryant, Grayson, and Hunter were moving the last of their possessions out of the cabin tomorrow, which meant we could move in once we cleaned the place. Three wolves and four pups in the small space had created some difficulties when it came to maintaining the cabin.

After I finished work, I wandered along the path through the trees that led to the cabin. Grayson was packing up the last of their clothes. They'd been kind enough to leave all the kitchen stuff, and some furniture original to the cabin. And the bed. Logan had already bought sets of sheets for it. The new mattress was coming tomorrow. Logan had insisted on a new one after imagining what the three wolves got up to on the old one. The mating and the whelping.

"Only a few more things," Grayson said to me. "I'll sweep the floor when I'm done."

"Don't worry. Logan and I can handle the clean up."

"I hate to leave it all to you."

"Logan is particular. We'd be cleaning the place top to bottom regardless."

Grayson lifted some shirts off a shelf. "So ... Lucas tells me Logan is an Alpha. I can give you some advice on that."

"You and Bryant."

"Our mating is special when it's just the two of us."

I furrowed my brow. "It's not always all three of you?"

"No, we take time with each other separately too. Mating with another Alpha is different. More primal. Sometimes more aggressive." He shrugged. "Sometimes sweet too."

I smiled. I'm not sure if Logan spanking me would be considered aggressive or sweet. It was done lovingly. And it made me feel good. I'd seeded the sheets beneath me many times.

"We're the same."

Grayson folded a pair of jeans and put them in a box. "Lucas also told us Logan was born an Omega. That his scent won't be Alpha. I want you to know, I respect that."

"Thank you, Grayson. He's my Alpha … and that's all there is to it."

"Good for you for following your heart. If Bryant, Hunter, and I hadn't done that, we would be in a much different situation. Our polyamorous relationship has brought us incredible joy."

"And brought you pups too."

Grayson looked up at me. "Is that a concern with Logan not identifying as an Omega?"

"Even if he didn't, he's passed breeding age."

Grayson scrubbed at his stubble as he studied me. "You know … Hunter would do it."

I felt my eyebrows peak. "Do what?"

"Carry a pup for you."

"Are you serious?" I took a step toward him.

"I'll ask him. Just a warning, though. I've heard you could end up with twins."

I couldn't contain the grin that spread across my face. "That would be fine."

Grayson laughed. "You say that until you've experienced it." He hoisted the box into his arms and headed for the door. "I'll talk to Hunter and Bryant. You talk to Logan."

I sat on the edge of the bed as Grayson left.

Logan had said he needed to think about it. I didn't want to push him but the possibility of having a surrogate I knew was an amazing carrier was something that needed to be discussed.

I went back to my house and fired up my truck.

Fifteen minutes later, I was traveling up the West Creekside driveway. I hadn't asked for permission to set foot on their territory, but I hoped being Logan's mate was enough to keep me out of trouble. A few wolves raised their heads from their work, but no one approached me.

I jogged up the steps of Logan's house.

Patrick opened the door. "Harlan. Good. Maybe you can calm Logan down."

I pushed past him. "What's wrong with him?"

"Something about having a pup. Tyler is talking to him."

I looked up the stairs. His scent was strong. I let it fill my senses. I'd been away from it for too many days. I jogged to the door I sensed him behind.

I knocked lightly and let myself in.

Logan was sitting on one of three beds. Tyler was sitting across from him. He had Logan's hands in his. I had to fight to calm my inner hackles.

Logan looked up at me, his face streaked with tears.

"Alpha." I took a seat beside him. Tyler released Logan's hands and rose to his feet.

"I'll leave you two alone," Tyler said. He touched Logan's shoulder. "My offer stands."

When we were alone, Logan began sobbing while he clutched my arm. Something it seemed he'd been doing for a while. His face was mottled and his nose running.

"I was thinking about what we talked about," he said after sucking in a shuddering breath.

"About pups?"

He leaned his head on my shoulder. "I want them with you—desperately."

"Are you upset we can't have them naturally?" I was taking a shot in the dark.

Logan's shoulders shook as he laughed half-heartedly. "I've been trying really hard."

I smiled and kissed his hair. "Yes, you have. Valiant effort. My ass thanks you."

"I would give you a pup if I could."

"I know you would." I wrapped my arm around his shoulders. "I was talking to Grayson." I gathered my courage. "He says he thinks Hunter would be a surrogate for us."

Logan sniffed and looked up at me. "So would Tyler. That's what we were talking about."

"So, you're entertaining it."

Logan nodded. "I want us to have a family that includes pups." He grasped my hand. "Except, our pup would carry your DNA but not mine. It would be Hunter or Tyler's."

"The pup would be ours, Logan. We'd raise it and love it. We'd be its protectors."

Logan stroked his hand up and down my thigh. "How would we choose?"

"I think we'd need to bring them both to a doctor. Although, we know Hunter is fertile. And he's super conscientious when he's pregnant. Organic and wild everything."

"Our pup would have lots of half-brothers and sisters in the pack. Do we want that?"

I sighed. "Maybe not. When they reach mating age, it would lessen their choices."

"But if he agrees, I don't think we should discount Hunter."

I gripped Logan's hands. "So, we're doing this?"

New tears streamed down Logan's face. "I think we might be."

THE FOUR OF US had been sitting in the waiting room for over an hour. Hunter and Tyler had been pulled aside for blood tests and I had looked through all the pamphlets in that time.

I had a better understanding of the procedure now. First, Hunter and Tyler would be taken in to see the doctor individually to discuss their health, including information about their heats.

Next, would be my turn. I'd have to produce a sample to test the effectiveness of my seed and then there would be a discussion. After that, we'd need to book another appointment.

I clung to Logan's hand. It had taken us 7 hours to drive here. We were both nervous and had barely slept in the days since we decided to go ahead with surrogacy.

When I'd phoned to make the appointment, I'd been told the doctor hadn't worked with many wolves. Our uniqueness bumped up the price.

I'd gone to Lucas to secure a loan that would take us a decade to pay off. Adam had intervened, taking Lucas aside. They had decided to give us the money from the pack's coffers for this first pup. If we wanted more pups, we would need to secure a loan from the pack.

"Hunter Black?"

Hunter raised his hand and popped up. He followed the person who had called him through a doorway. Logan and I had to separate our hands; they were becoming so sweaty as we waited. Hunter was in there for 30 minutes before he was swapped out with Tyler.

"Harlan Armstrong?"

I rose to my feet. "That's me."

"Follow me."

I looked at Logan. "Can he come with me?"

"Not this time. Your partner can come in with you when you see the doctor."

A small knot tightened in my stomach. I knew this was the part where I would have to give a sample of my seed. What if I couldn't perform? What if I was infertile?

I was led to a small room with a chair, a television, and a table covered in magazines and DVDs. I was directed to use a cup that had my name on it and to put the sample behind a small door in the wall where it would be collected by a technician.

The door closed and I sat down on the chair. This really would have been easier if Logan had come with me. I flipped through the magazines. They had a couple with males in them.

I set one on the table in front of me and opened the first page. It was an article I had no interest in reading. On the next page, a male in a hot pink G-string. Front and back. His ass was nice.

Logan's was better.

Flip to the next page. This was more interesting. A male dressed like a mechanic set against the background of a real repair shop. His coveralls open. His cock protruding, erect.

I unzipped my jeans and dug around in my underwear until I had my semi-hard cock in my hand. I started stroking it as I let my gaze wander over every detail of the model's body.

I could imagine Logan in an outfit like that, working on a motorcycle. I turned the page. The mechanic had lost his overalls completely and was leaning forward working on the tire of a car. They had a side view and a view from the back. His ass was round and muscular. Built for drilling a cock into you hard. He could probably lift me in his arms and spear me on it.

My cock throbbed in my hand. I spotted some lube packets on the table. I retrieved one, opened it, and squirted the contents into my hand. Every single one of the nerve endings came to life on my shaft as I used the slickness to pump it faster.

I turned the page and groaned. A picture of a male lying on his back, legs in the air, exposing his perfect hole. The photo on the opposing page—him fingering himself.

I grabbed the cup, my cock pulsing, and shot straight into it, filling the bottom to an acceptable level. I reached for a packet of handy wipes, cleaned up, and closed my jeans.

After putting the cup behind the little door, I returned to the waiting room.

"That was quick," Logan said, smirking at me.

"They had some good stuff back there."

"Harlan and Logan?"

We gripped each other's hands and rose to our feet. We passed Tyler on his way back to the waiting room. He winked at us and whispered, "Good luck."

Once in an office, we took seats in front of a desk with a doctor on the other side who was looking at his computer screen. He moused back and forth and then looked at us.

"So, you want to be parents."

"Very much," Logan said as I nodded.

"Well, you seem to have two very good candidates for surrogate. I would, however, recommend you use Hunter. He's already had two successful pregnancies."

"We're concerned about the mating options for our pup if we use Hunter," I said. "There aren't many wolves in the area. Having four siblings and two cousins in the pack limits options."

"There are other packs, though."

"I come from a different pack," Logan said. "The same one as Tyler."

"So … you and Harlan would be considered rivals?"

"We're fated. It doesn't matter."

"Do you have family in your pack, Logan?"

"None."

The doctor leaned back in his chair. "Then Tyler might be the better option considering your concerns. His blood work came back clear, and he has no hereditary family illnesses." He looked at his computer and clicked on something. "The report on your sample is back, Harlan. Your swimmers are plentiful and strong. I doubt we'll have a problem from your end."

I hadn't realized I'd been holding my breath. I released it and gripped tighter to Logan's hand.

"I have to ask, though," the doctor said. "You seem very young for starting a family, Harlan. Are you sure this is something you want to take on? It's a lot of responsibility, a child."

"We're mated for life," I said. "If Logan were younger, we might be with pup already. We're just taking a different path. We'll face any challenges together as fated mates."

"As long as you're sure," the doctor replied.

"What happens next?" Logan asked.

"Well, we send Tyler home with some drugs to stimulate his egg production. Then we'll book a follow-up appointment to harvest the eggs. We'll need another sample from you that day, Harlan. Once we have that, we'll fertilize the eggs and see which ones take."

"And then Tyler …."

"He'll come back for another appointment 5 days later where we'll implant the fertilized eggs."

"And when will we know if it's working?" I asked.

"Tyler will need to come back a week later so we can do a pregnancy test."

Logan leaned against me and shifted his hand from my hand to my arm. He was gripping me so tight, I had to stroke his hand to get him to relax. He reached for a box of tissues on the desk.

"Alpha." I turned his face toward me. He was crying. "Are you ready for this?"

Logan nodded. "So ready."

"All right." I stood with Logan still clinging to my arm. "We'd like to proceed."

"I think you have excellent chances of being successful." The doctor went to his door and opened it for us. "Send Tyler down here and speak to the receptionist about payment."

Both Hunter and Tyler were looking at us expectantly when we returned to the waiting room. Logan rushed to Tyler and pulled him up and into his arms. "Thank you."

Hunter patted Tyler on the ass. "Go. The doctor will want to see you again."

I let Logan explain to Hunter why we had chosen Tyler while I went to arrange payment. Lucas had given me a massive wad of paper money. I'd put it in my bank account rather than bring it to the appointment. Humans didn't use cash as readily as wolves did.

I hoped they'd accept a check.

They did.

I sank into a seat beside Logan and the full force of what we were doing hit me—hard. I was taking a serious leap away from my youth with a fated mate twice my age. We would be bound together by a pup or pups. Grayson was right. Sometimes more than one embryo thrived.

I sucked in a long breath. This is what I wanted. This is what *we* wanted. Logan was my mate and I loved him. We'd yet to perform the claiming ceremony but we were committed to each other. Having pups was an extension of that commitment. I squeezed Logan's thigh.

"I love you," I said.

"You're my world, Harlan."

"We're really doing this."

"You'll make an amazing sire."

"So will you, Alpha." I nudged him with my shoulder. "Our pup is going to think you're cooler. I'm a lowly plumber. You bring bad ass motorcycles to life."

"You ride them *too*."

I chuckled. "Not the same."

"Okay, I'm set." Tyler walked toward us with a plastic bag I knew contained all the syringes he would need to inject himself with a cocktail of drugs. He was doing us an incredible favor. Not only putting up with the hormonal changes but carrying a pup for us for 8 weeks.

And he'd be giving the pup up to us.

It was a lot to ask of anyone. We'd promised him he would be involved in the pup's life. That the pup would know Tyler was its carrier. That he was essentially part of our family.

We'd spent some time with Tyler and Patrick, with me getting to know Tyler better. He was taking the responsibility seriously, reassuring us he wouldn't be doing anything reckless like riding his motorcycles. And that he'd eat well and get plenty of rest. He was going to behave himself.

Unexpectedly, Patrick had a lot of questions. In fact, he had grilled us. He and Tyler might not be mates but there was a strong bond between them. Enough of one that Tyler had given Patrick a veto over the whole decision. He wouldn't have done it without Patrick's approval.

The trip back home was quiet. Everyone was tired. It had been a long and eventful day. We dropped off Tyler and Patrick, only letting Tyler mount the steps of his house after hugging him.

This was going to change all our lives.

Me, Logan, Tyler … and Patrick.

Chapter Eight | Logan

The drive into Metro City seemed to take longer this time. All four of us were feeling anxious. Tyler had been injecting himself with the drugs. I knew that for sure because his mood had turned foul, and he was forever complaining about headaches and tiredness.

He'd been told these were all possible side effects of the drugs. Today was the moment of truth as to whether Tyler's body had produced an abundance of eggs. It was going to be an uncomfortable day for him. They would give him pain medication and a sedative to help him through the collection of the eggs, but a rear entry collection had challenges.

We arrived at the office at noon so Tyler could be prepped.

Patrick had insisted on coming with us.

When Tyler was called in, Patrick leaped up, wrapped Tyler in his arms, and hugged him tight. He whispered something in Tyler's ear that made Tyler smile and whisper back to him.

I looked down at Harlan's and my joined hands.

It was obvious, Patrick and Tyler weren't telling us everything.

Patrick reluctantly released Tyler and came back to sit beside us. There were tears in his eyes. I reached for his thigh and placed my hand on it. "He's going to be all right."

Patrick nodded. "I know. He's resilient."

Time dragged by until Harlan was called in to give his contribution for our pup. He squeezed my hand before disappearing behind the door to the back rooms. It took him longer this time. The monumental reason he was jerking off was presumably on his mind.

He looked worried when he came back to me.

"What's wrong?"

"I hope I gave enough."

"They don't need much."

Harlan sighed and rolled his shoulders. "Stressful."

"I'm sure you did fine. I've never known you to be deficient in that respect."

Patrick shifted and huffed beside me.

I turned to him. "Are you sure you're okay with this?"

"Tyler wants the experience of whelping a pup. One he can bond with."

"And that doesn't sit well with you?"

"It's what he wants."

Harlan tugged on my arm. "Leave him. Let him sort through his emotions."

Tyler emerged from the back, looking groggy. Patrick bounded toward him and placed his arm around Tyler's shoulders to guide him to us. We'd already made our next appointment.

Almost the entire drive home, Patrick kept his arm around Tyler. When he wasn't holding him, Tyler had his head leaning on Patrick's shoulder.

A few days later we received a phone call.

"Logan?"

"Speaking."

"This is *Metro City Infertility Clinic*. We have news for you. Three of Tyler's eggs have been successfully fertilized. You have some decisions to make."

Harlan tugged on my arm. "Let me put you on speaker." My love crowded closer to me, curiosity in his eyes. "Three of Tyler's eggs were fertilized."

"We need to know how many you want to implant," the technician continued.

We'd talked about it. Tyler had offered to carry twins. Grayson and Bryant had warned us that twins were a handful and we had experienced the mayhem in their new home firsthand.

But they had *two* sets of twins.

"You mentioned we could freeze some," Harlan said.

"Yes, we could do that, but it'll cost you a lot more money. Keep in mind the implanted embryos might not all thrive."

"Can we decide when we come in?" I asked. "We need to talk to Tyler."

Harlan nodded. Tyler needed to be part of the discussion. Half the genetic material to create these little miracles was his. He had a say in the creation of his pup or pups.

"Yes, you can do that. Be ready with an answer, though."

"We'll talk on the ride there," Harlan replied.

"See you Thursday."

"Yes. Thank you." I hung up the phone. "Thursday," I said to Harlan. "Our lives might change on Thursday. We might be expecting a pup or pups."

Harlan gathered me up in his arms and kissed me. "We might be sires."

I went to sleep that night dreaming of our pups running around our feet, barking, and leaping about, chasing their tails and yipping at each other.

It was telling that there was more than one.

THE NEXT APPOINTMENT went well. Patrick insisted on coming with us again. This time holding Tyler's hand all the way to the city, occasionally whispering to him.

We couldn't help but notice the quick peck on the cheek Patrick gave Tyler before he was taken into the back. We'd made a bold decision. Patrick was concerned.

On the drive to the appointment, we discussed the number of embryos. We'd told Tyler as soon as we knew the number of successful fertilizations, so he had time to think about it.

We'd let him decide. We knew where our hearts lay, but ultimately, it wasn't up to us. Tyler knew how much his body could bear. How much discomfort he was willing to put up with. Harlan and I had cried tears of relief and joy when Tyler said to implant all three.

When we'd arrived at the appointment and told the doctor of our decision, he'd seen no reason for us to be concerned about Tyler's body being able to handle three pups.

The whole way home, the truck was silent except for Patrick and Tyler talking quietly to each other when Tyler hadn't fallen asleep on Patrick's shoulder.

After dropping the two wolves off, again expressing out incredible thanks to Tyler … to both of them really, we headed to our little cabin in the woods. We were in the height of summer, so we didn't need a fire. The cabin was stuffy and warm, so we left the door open.

Harlan lay down on the bed. It had been a long drive, even though Harlan and I had taken turns. I had spent most of the ride home thinking. Tyler had been implanted with embryos containing Harlan's seed today. In a week's time, we would know if Harlan was pregnant.

7 weeks after that, we'd have pups.

The Omega inside me was screaming to be a part of the process.

I lay down beside Harlan and rolled toward him, to cuddle against him.

The words formed on my tongue, hung there, and tortured me for a few moments. I wanted to say them and not say them at the same time. I wanted what I was going to ask, but I feared it.

I pushed past the barricade in my mind.

"I want you to mate with me."

Harlan turned his head to face me. "What?"

"Tyler might be pregnant today."

Harlan rose on one elbow. "He might be. Why does that involve me mating with you?"

I wasn't sure if I was crazy for wanting this. I just knew I wanted it. "If I was younger and we mated tonight, you might put a pup in me."

Understanding washed over Harlan's gaze. "You want it to seem as if you're the one having our pup. That the timing of our mating coincides with Tyler's pregnancy."

I nodded. Maybe I was insane.

"You've seeded Tyler today. I want to feel a part of that. I want you to seed me even though I can't get pregnant. I want to be able to imagine Tyler's pregnancy is mine."

"My sweet Alpha." Harlan kissed my forehead and stroked my cheek. "Are you sure?"

"Please, Harlan. I long to feel you inside me. Caressing me—flooding me with your seed."

Harlan cupped my face. "I love you."

"I love you too." I trembled in his grasp.

He fingered the sleeve of my t-shirt and then my shorts. He hauled my knee onto his hip and rolled me until I was on top of him. I loved looking down at him, his thick lashes fluttering. But tonight, it would be the reverse. Tonight, Harlan would be above me. Sinking into *me*.

I stripped off my shirt and struggled to remove his. It got caught on his chin, but we soon had it off. Normally, that would have started us laughing, but tonight was different.

I was about to accept something I had never accepted before.

Harlan knew this was monumental for me.

Straddling Harlan's hips, Harlan unbuttoned and unzipped my shorts. I stood, keeping my balance, and removed them and my underwear, making the bed wobble.

This time, I did get a small smile from my fated mate.

I kneeled, straddling Harlan's shins, and tugged off his shorts and underwear. As I ascended his body, he kicked his legs, freeing them from the restriction.

I wrapped my arms around his neck and kissed him. The kiss of two lovers about to take a step into something special. His hands skimmed my spine and then settled on my ass.

He turned me slowly until I was under him.

"My beautiful Alpha," he whispered.

I gripped the back of his neck as he scraped his descended canines back and forth over my claiming area between my neck and shoulder. He hummed as he licked and nibbled at it.

My hips undulated and I wrapped my legs around his waist. His cock was hard as it jammed repeatedly against my belly, his precum dampening my skin.

I wanted him. I wanted all of him.

His cock prodded lower. First against the base of my cock. Then my balls. Then the crease of my ass. He licked and sucked my earlobe, growling low and quiet, but thunderous.

"Mate with me," I whispered.

Harlan lined up his cock against my hole with one hand. There was a slight burn as Harlan's cockhead breached my tight ring. It felt exquisite to have him so close to me.

He slid higher into me, still sucking on my ear—and my neck.

He kissed my cheek.

"This doesn't make you any less an Alpha," he whispered.

I nodded, tears gathering in my eyes. He was right. Harlan was an Alpha with promise. Someday, he would take his place among the top of the pack. Maybe even as pack leader.

Yet, every night, he welcomed me into his arms to seed him.

I wrapped my arms around him, thrilled by everything he was offering. His hips pumped against me, filling my insides. I'd never felt closer to him.

I loved this wolf with my entire being.

Harlan grunted in my ear. "I want to be yours."

The claiming ceremony.

It was fitting.

"And I yours," I responded.

Harlan's hips increased in pace and then he stopped. I could feel the swell of a knot against my hole. He licked my claiming area … and bit down.

I howled as the pain cascaded through me. He sucked in mouthfuls of my blood and jammed his cock higher, forcing the knot past my ring. Sparks of ecstasy lit up my mind.

I closed my eyes to enjoy them and the feel of Harlan's knotted cock filling me; the swollen flesh at its base pressing deliciously against my prostate.

It was my turn. I hauled his shoulder closer to me and ran my tongue over my canines. They had descended when Harlan bit me. I found the spot, inhaling its unique scent.

I saw red and pierced his flesh, biting into him.

He released me from his canines and howled in response. The telepathic connection that had been lingering moments before snapped into existence. His thoughts of love for me overwhelmed me. I unclamped my jaws and joined him in a song of fated mates—claimed fated mates.

The rest of the East Creekside pack could be heard howling into the night in response to our claiming. I wasn't just one with Harlan. I was part of a pack that accepted Harlan and me.

Rejoiced in our union.

Harlan's knot softened as I whimpered, wanting the warmth to fill me.

He growled and flooded me with his seed.

I HAD TWO NEW motorcycles to work on this week. It was difficult to take my mind off Tyler's impending appointment tomorrow when we'd find out if he was pregnant.

Right now, he was busy doing an oil change on an old Buick. Patrick wouldn't let him do anything strenuous. I watched him for a moment. He didn't look any different.

Then the most joyous thing happened. Tyler rushed from the bay and flew into the bathroom. I could hear him retching and throwing up in the toilet. It was the sign we'd all been waiting for.

Patrick skidded in front of the bathroom doorway after running to it. He rushed in and I could hear him speaking to Tyler. I didn't want to interrupt. This was their journey too.

My heart fluttered around, beyond excited. Our dream was coming true. I wished I could call Harlan, but he was out on a job. I knew where, though.

I jogged over to the bathroom door. Patrick was squatted beside Tyler, rubbing his back. "Can I borrow your truck? I want to tell Harlan that Tyler is pregnant."

Patrick looked up at me. "You know where the keys are." Before I walked away, he rose to his feet. "I guess congratulations are in order."

"For all of us."

Patrick grunted but his face remained neutral. He went back to soothing Tyler. It was hard to read Patrick. Ultimately, I knew he wanted Tyler to be happy above all else.

The old truck sprung to life as I turned the key. It was a short drive. At the far end of the township but less than 10 minutes. As I pulled up outside the house, sweat beaded on my forehead and I felt clammy. Even my hands were sweating. I chalked it up to being excited.

I leaped from the truck and knocked on the door of the house. A woman answered.

"Can I help you?"

"I'm here to see Harlan. I'm his mate."

"Oh, come in." She stepped back from the doorway. "Harlan has been telling me all about you. I'm so glad he found someone." She extended her hand. "I'm Linda."

"Logan."

"Come, come." She placed her hand on my shoulder and escorted me down the hallway. "We're putting in a bathroom downstairs." She pointed at the stairs. "He's down there."

"Thank you." I jogged down the stairs and listened for the sounds of Harlan working. The basement was immense. The smell of some kind of adhesive overshadowed his scent.

"Harlan?"

Harlan popped his head out from around a corner at the far end of a hallway.

"Hey, Logan." He furrowed his brow. "What's wrong? Tyler all right?"

I grinned at him. "At the moment, he has his head in the toilet."

Harlan laughed, raced toward me, and caught me in his arms, swinging me around. "We're pregnant?" He set me down and kissed me, then looked over his shoulder. "Linda, we're pregnant!"

The woman I had met at the door trundled down the stairs. "What?"

"Tyler. He's throwing up."

Linda clapped her hands together. "Oh, that is wonderful news. Starting a family already."

"Us wolves don't tend to wait before trying for pups."

"Now, how long until he has them? You told me but I just can't believe it."

"It'll be 7 weeks now," I said.

"Oh my, that is fast."

Harlan couldn't stop grinning. I grabbed his chin and planted a kiss on him. He was adorable when he was excited. I went from elated to thrown off. I'd almost lost my balance.

I gripped Harlan's sleeve.

He grabbed my other arm. "Are you all right?"

"Just excited. Got a bit dizzy."

"Do you need to sit down?"

I shook my head. "No, I'm fine. I should get back to work."

"I could drive you."

"I have Patrick's truck." I patted his hand. "I'm fine. See you in a few hours. We'll have a full spread of food to celebrate. Maybe some champagne."

Harlan cupped my face. "I'll pick some up on my way to grab you."

I leaned into another kiss from my Alpha wolf, then followed Linda upstairs. When I returned to the service station, Tyler was back under the car, completing his job.

"Are you feeling better?" I asked him.

"For now. Constant state of queasy, though." He wiped his hands on a grubby cloth. "I think we know what the result of that pregnancy test is going to be tomorrow."

I smirked at him. "Unless you ate some bad meat."

Tyler laughed. "Patrick has been bringing me fresh game every day."

"He's being very attentive."

"Annoyingly so." Tyler smiled shyly. "But I appreciate him."

Whatever their relationship status, I was glad Patrick was around to keep tabs on Tyler. Harlan and I didn't want to crowd our surrogate, but we wanted the best for him.

I went back to working on the motorcycle I had been disassembling for hours. I liked the predictability of the order of the process. I could take an engine apart in my sleep.

I gripped the workbench as a wave of warmth ran from my gut to my face. I let it pass and went back to work. Maybe I was coming down with something. Unusual for a wolf. We weren't prone to the viruses that plagued humans—especially their offspring.

More likely, the excitement of the day.

I was glad when Harlan arrived to pick me up. I wanted to be home with him.

"You actually picked up champagne." I lifted the bottle in the front seat. He'd also bought some blueberries and quails' eggs. It seemed we were spoiling ourselves.

"Not every day you find out you have a pup coming."

I held his hand as he drove up the driveway to the compound. Lucas, Adam, and a few other wolves were standing on Lucas' porch as we pulled up.

Harlan had obviously put out the word through the telepathic link.

Carina and Reese were making their way from their houses to join the others. We were rushed by wolves hugging us and giving their congratulations.

It was overwhelming.

I still wasn't feeling right. I leaned against Harlan and whined. I wanted to be in his arms. Not among a crowd of exuberant wolves. I inhaled the scent of him to calm myself.

I tugged on his arm as my cock throbbed.

I *needed* to be alone with him.

Harlan must have caught the scent of my arousal because he whipped his head around to look at me, a mix of surprise and desire in his eyes.

I whined again. This time, he made our excuses, telling the wolves that we had plans for celebrating we wanted to get to. There were a few understanding looks.

All the way back to the cabin, I was only aware of my Alpha.

Nothing existed outside of him.

The bag of groceries was abandoned on the kitchen counter, and we crashed onto the bed together, our lips connecting and seeking something we had only pursued once before.

I wanted him all over me. All over and inside me. My desire to revisit the one time he had mated with me was strong. I wanted to feel that rush again—feel him fill me.

Harlan unbuttoned and unzipped my jeans and yanked them off, discarding them at the end of the bed. My cock was hard and aching. A drizzle of precum landed on my belly.

My lover chased it, licking it up.

He stopped what he was doing and looked up at me.

"Your scent and taste are different."

I closed my eyes and played through how I had felt today. My face felt hot again, and I could feel the copious slickness leaking onto the inside of my ass cheeks.

Harlan kissed my stomach. "Your belly is puffy." His eyes opened wide as he looked at me. "Logan, what's going on? My urge to mate with you is off the charts."

I brushed my hand through Harlan's hair.

I knew what it was.

"I'm in heat, Alpha."

Chapter Nine | Harlan

I sat on the bed beside Logan, staring at him, unsure what to say. He'd just dropped some bombshell-level news. I wasn't sure what it meant for us and our desire for pups.

"You haven't had a heat in over a year," I said. "You told me that."

"I haven't." Logan set his hand on his stomach. "I don't know why it's happening. Maybe Tyler's pregnancy triggered my body into having one final go around."

My mind was slammed with images of Logan pregnant.

I touched his thigh. "What does that mean for us?"

Logan lay his hand on mine. "That this might be the last time I can give you a pup."

I caught and held his gaze. "But is that what you want?"

"I *want* to give you the world, Harlan." Logan stroked his hand along my jawline and into my hair, tickling the top of my ear with his fingers. "I *want* our lives to be filled with love."

"You want to try for a pup?"

Logan's shoulders rose and fell as his breathing deepened. There was an internal struggle going on. I could see it in the way he searched my eyes. "I can ask Patrick for some time off after we take Tyler to tomorrow's appointment so we can have some time to ourselves."

I gripped his leg, ready to launch myself at him and kiss him.

"Is that a *yes*?" I asked.

Logan smiled, nodded, and cupped my face in both hands. "Yes, Alpha. I want a pup with you." He squealed and tipped backward as I flew at his lips, half grinning—half kissing.

We rolled around in each other's arms in a state of euphoria at what we had decided.

"Can we start now?" I asked, beyond delirious.

Logan pressed his forehead to mine. "Being pregnant is going to be a big deal for me."

"You'll always be my Alpha." He had to know that I would still consider him to be an Alpha even if his belly was swollen with a pup. "A pregnancy wouldn't change that."

Logan raked his fingers into my hair and kissed me, taking from my lips every assurance I had given him. I knew he believed me. "Put a pup in me, Alpha."

Words I'd longed to hear. I stripped down, my cock aching to fill my Alpha with my seed. Logan rolled me onto my back, straddled me, and gripped both our cocks in his hand.

He gazed down at me as he stroked both shafts—slow and easy. There was incredible love in his eyes. He rubbed his thumb across each slit, coating his skin, and lifted it to his lips.

He sucked his thumb into his mouth, closed his eyes, and moaned.

My cock jumped. He fell forward, one arm to the left of my head, his other still on our cocks. He dangled his tongue in my mouth. I closed my lips around it and sucked. He withdrew.

Logan's gaze never left my eyes as he switched to caressing my cock alone. He rose to his knees and moved forward. With one hand around behind him, he guided my cock to his hole.

He groaned and swore as he took me all the way in. His ass came to rest on my thighs. He didn't move except to play with his cock, stroking it.

I set my hands on his hips.

"I love you, Alpha," I said.

"I meant what I said. I want to give you the world." Logan started moving, lifting off, and then lowering himself onto me. He rode me slow and steady, increasing my lust for him.

I reached for his cock and pumped it.

He went from gentle movements atop me to bouncing on my hips, compressing my balls with each down thrust. He growled as his ass closed tighter around my cock.

He came down hard on me, grunted, and spilled his seed on my stomach. I gathered up his seed in one hand and continued to stroke his cock slowly.

He liked it when I prolonged the attention.

Logan jammed his ass against me harder and faster. He let out an incredible howling song as my cock jumped and pulsed inside him, filling him with seed.

He milked every drop out of me, clamping down on my cock, and rising and falling at a leisurely pace until he sat still on my hips and leaned forward to kiss me.

"Be prepared to do that all night," he whispered against his lips.

"Challenge accepted." I grinned, kissed him, and rolled him onto his back.

WE HAD THE WHOLE TRIP to the appointment to tell Tyler that we were trying for our own pup. The thing we were concerned about—Patrick's reaction. The possibility of Logan becoming pregnant in no way changed our arrangement with Tyler. We were prepared to have a houseful of pups. I had spoken to Lucas since everyone had heard Logan's song that we were trying for a pup.

He had promised to have a home built for us if we were willing to accommodate some of his pups as soon as they reached the age of eighteen. We had agreed.

Tyler's appointment confirmed that he was indeed pregnant. We had launched into a huddled hug, all four of us. Even Patrick was laughing, excited.

It was during the ride home that Logan opened the discussion. "I have news," he said as he looked over his shoulder into the backseat.

Tyler gripped the back of Logan's seat and leaned forward.

"You don't want to work for us anymore?" Patrick asked.

"No." Logan shook his head. "Never that. I love my job. But I am going to need a few days off. Harlan and I have something we need to be doing."

There was silence from the backseat.

"I'm in heat," Logan revealed. "We're trying for a pup."

"But you already have three pups coming," Patrick said. "Tyler is pregnant."

Tyler was quiet. I could sense him falling back into his seat.

"What does this mean for Tyler?" Patrick asked. "Do you *not* want these pups anymore?"

"Nothing changes," I replied. "We want a house full of pups."

"Jeezus." Patrick glared at me in the rearview mirror. "Way to throw everything off. Tyler is going to put his body through a pregnancy with triplets. You better not change your mind."

"Not a chance," Logan said. "We promise. Nothing changes."

"I'd have them either way," Tyler said to Patrick. "We could raise them together."

I chanced a glance in the rearview mirror. Patrick was kissing Tyler's head. I couldn't make out what they said after that. Every word was in a hushed whisper.

It was obvious there was a level of love between them.

Two Omegas, though. They'd likely never be able to produce their own pups.

It was a cruel genetic fault in the wolf shifter physiology.

Patrick said Logan could have three days off when we dropped them at home. We spent those three days in bed, only stopping our mating to sleep, recover, drink copious amounts of water, and feed on the game Carina provided for us. The whole pack was invested in our success.

I rolled over and kissed Logan's shoulder during our last morning together. We had to return to work in the next couple of hours. We were both too sore to mate again.

"Good morning, Alpha," I said.

"Mmm," Logan hummed and turned to face me. He gave me a slow kiss. "A bath before work is in order. To clean up *and* to give my poor ass some soothing warmth."

I smiled against his lips. "Do you think it worked?"

"We'll know in a few days." Logan touched my chin. "I'll be fine to continue by tonight."

I laughed. "You're right. You are a stallion. I'm surprised I kept up."

"I'm determined."

His lips felt warm against mine. I took his mouth, caressing his lips, and seeking companionship with his tongue. I'd never tire of kissing Logan. He was my weakness.

I loved and worshipped him.

FIVE DAYS LATER when I arrived to pick Logan up from work, Patrick directed me to the bathroom. Logan was on his knees in front of the toilet, his face resting on the porcelain bowl.

I couldn't contain the grin that spread across my face as Logan vomited.

"I'm here, Alpha." I rubbed his back and waited for a reprieve from the retching.

Logan rested his head on the arm he had stretched along the bowl.

"Not sure if I love you or hate you right now," he said. "This is brutal."

"How long have you been throwing up?"

"On and off, starting this morning. Tyler says he was the same. Must be your seed's fault."

I smirked. "Potent stuff."

"Ha ha."

I pulled some paper towels off the roll and wet them under some cold water. I used it to hold against Logan's forehead. He sighed and hummed which meant it must feel good.

After what seemed like twenty minutes, Logan hadn't thrown up again.

"Should I take you home now?" I asked.

Logan hauled himself to his feet. "Please. I need to lie down."

"We'll pick up some ginger on the way home. I'll make you some tea."

"That helped Tyler," Patrick said as he leaned in the bathroom doorway. "Add some lemon and honey. It makes it taste better. I let a big pot simmer on the stove every night. For during the day, you should pick up an insulated hot drink container. I made sure Tyler always had one."

"Thanks, Patrick," I replied. "I'm glad you have it worked out already. I have no idea what I'm doing. Not sure what to expect. I'm glad Tyler is almost two weeks ahead of us."

"His feet are swelling as well," Patrick shared. "I have to rub them every night."

"That's very gallant of you," Logan said.

"He's my best friend. I want him to be comfortable."

Friend.

Right.

"Let's get you home," I said to Logan.

"I want you to see Tyler first. He's showing."

I hadn't seen Tyler on the way in. When we returned to the bay, he was hovering over an engine. When he saw us, he straightened, put his hand on the small of his back, and stretched.

His belly was round. Not the tight abs I had grown accustomed to when picking up Logan. Tyler tended to work in a sleeveless white t-shirt, showing off his incredible muscles.

Now the shirt was stretched slightly to accommodate his pregnancy.

I approached him. "How have you been feeling?" I asked.

"Tired and sore." He set a wrench down and placed his hand on his stomach. "Otherwise, I'm doing as well as can be expected. Appetite is good. Throwing up has stopped."

An emotion of gratitude bubbled up in me.

"You have no idea how much we appreciate this," I said. "Those pups will have everything they need to thrive. You have our promise."

Logan gripped my arm. "I tell Tyler that every day. I've become annoying."

"The clinic phoned me," Tyler said to me. "They want me to come in for an appointment in two weeks so they can do an ultrasound. Make sure all three pups are all right."

"We'll drive you," I said much too quickly.

Tyler laughed. "Obviously. It'll be our first look at the pups."

"I have the details for the appointment," Logan said.

I left the garage feeling elated. Tyler's pregnancy was progressing without problems, and we were going to see our pups in a couple of weeks for the very first time.

Logan and I fell asleep in each other's arms that night after talking about how excited we were about what we might see. All the wiggly little bodies and paws. And their heartbeats.

It was everything we had imagined. As Tyler was stretched out on the examining table, the technician moving a wand over his stomach, three little bodies came into view. One was smaller than the other two, but all had strong hearts and looked well-formed. Patrick was the one to insist we get a printout for both parties. He intended to pin the image to the wall in their bedroom.

Tyler was so tired, he just smiled at the suggestion and reached for Patrick's hand. We left them alone so Tyler could clean the gel off himself and redress.

Three weeks later, in the middle of the night, we got the call. Tyler was in the process of whelping the pups. By this time, Logan's belly was round and beautiful.

I kissed it every night before we went to sleep.

We arrived at Patrick's and Tyler's house. It was full of commotion. I wanted to jog up the stairs to the bedrooms, but I paced myself and went at Logan's speed.

We found Patrick sitting on a bed with his back against the headboard, Tyler's furry head in his lap. He was petting Tyler's muzzle from one end of his jawline to the other. Tyler had chosen to whelp in wolf form. The doctor had indicated it might be easier on him.

We sat on the bed across from the one Tyler and Patrick were on. An elderly Omega was fussing with a stack of towels. Setting three on a table and placing two under Tyler's back end.

Tyler's body tensed and he whined.

Patrick whispered, "Breathe," to him until Tyler's body relaxed. His hand moved from Tyler's muzzle to his shoulder, caressing it. "You can do this, Omega."

I gripped Logan's hand.

Patrick calling Tyler *Omega* was a term of intense endearment coming from another Omega.

These pups were going to be surrounded by love.

Tyler whined and lifted his head, looking down the length of his body. The elderly Omega parted the hair at Tyler's rear end and kept her hands there. A massive convulsion from Tyler and a tiny, mottled sac emerged into the Omega's hands. She pulled the sac casing away from the little body, grabbed a towel, and started rubbing the lifeless pup.

She passed the bundle of towel and pup to me.

"Start rubbing, sire. Give little puffs of air into its nose if it doesn't start to cry soon."

I rubbed the pup's back.

"Harder," the Omega barked at me. "Unless you don't want it to draw its first breath."

I was rougher with the pup until it started making tiny squeaking noises. I held the towel away from its face so Logan could take a peek. Before he had a chance to touch its damp furry head, he was handed his own pup to work on. Before long we had two breathing, restless pups.

I inhaled. Both were perfect female Omegas.

"Find a teat for them," the elderly Omega instructed. "The first milk is most important."

We moved closer to Tyler. Patrick reached down and exposed a teat for me. I placed the pup on it, holding her there until she latched on. Patrick did the same for Logan.

The elderly Omega passed me the third pup. A small male Alpha. Much smaller than his sisters. I handed him to Patrick. He looked at me with eyebrows raised, eyes wide.

I was entrusting him with a huge responsibility.

He took the tiny package and rubbed him until the pup started complaining. Once he had the male pup latched on, Tyler lifted his head, sniffed each one, and began licking them.

The agreement was that Tyler would keep the pups until they were weaned, feeding on meat mash well, and in the process of being house-trained. Likely by the time the pup Logan was carrying was at least 6 weeks old. Then our little cabin would become extremely full.

Patrick stayed where he was, supporting Tyler's head, and petting him.

We kissed the back of each of our little pups and snuck out, so we didn't wake Tyler. We'd come by in a few days after he'd had a chance to rest. Whelping three pups had not been easy on him. We knew he and the pups were in good hands with Patrick.

"They're beautiful," Logan said as we lay in bed early the next morning. We hadn't slept much. He smiled and nudged me. "Even though they're all brindle like their sire."

"I thought at least one of them would have come out grey like Tyler." I rolled and kissed Logan's cheek. "I hope ours is black like you."

"I'd prefer if the pup was the same color as its siblings."

I sighed. "Yeah, that makes sense. We don't want it to feel different than the others." I swept my hand up Logan's t-shirt. There were two wet marks above his nipples. I lifted myself off the mattress and straddled Logan's thighs. He grinned up at me.

"What are you doing?"

I folded Logan's shirt up until his chest was exposed. His once tight nipples were pink and puffy with beads of white milk at the tips. They could wait a moment. I started with his swollen belly, brushing my hands all over it until Logan sighed and shifted beneath me.

Logan raised his hands above his head and bit his bottom lip as he looked at me. I kept his shirt out of my way as I leaned down and took one of his nipples into my mouth. Logan groaned as I sucked hard on it, the milk spraying onto my tongue. I cupped his other soft pec. They had filled out deliciously, preparing for our pup. Logan jammed his hand into my hair and grabbed a clump of it as I switched sides. I kept myself balanced as I worked on his pants with both hands.

Once I had them undone, I reluctantly abandoned his leaking nipples; my second favorite taste. My first and third being his cock and his mouth. Right now, I was headed for his cock.

I tugged his pants down and gripped the base of his shaft, slipping his foreskin away to expose his glistening cockhead. I took my first taste. Combined with the milk, I was in heaven.

My skill had improved significantly from my first awkward attempt at giving Logan head in that sleeping bag. It was hard to believe that had only been a few months ago.

Logan swore, his hips bucking up as he flooded my throat with his glorious seed.

Now, we were a family with three pups and one more on the way.

All before my twentieth birthday.

I felt blessed to be living a life with Logan.

In love.

My Alpha.

Chapter Ten | Logan

Harlan was busy cleaning the cabin before Tyler and Patrick's arrival. Not sure why. All four of our pups were going to be tramping around making a mess in no time.

I had whelped our little black pup 6 weeks ago. It was a milestone but eclipsed by his birth. There was little chance we'd ever cry with exhilaration that hard again. The emotion of having a pup we had created on our own was monumental. He was a perfect little Omega male whose head and breath smelled amazing. We often lay on the bed simply watching him sleep.

We had just started Reese Jr. on mashed meat mixed with my chest milk. He was taking well to it, and the change in his food gave me a break from chest feeding him every two hours.

Today was the day Tyler and Patrick would bring the three pups they had raised to date to our cabin—and leave them with us to become their primary protectors.

I tried to prepare myself for the emotions that were going to be ruling us all. We'd been visiting the pups every day at the house Tyler and Patrick lived in. During the past week, they'd been bringing the pups to our cabin to get them used to the different environment.

In a few hours, Tyler and Patrick would be driving back to their home without them.

I caught the pups' scent as they made their way through the forest to our cabin. Their progress was slow. Both because their legs were short and because they were naturally curious.

I set little Reese on the bed as Harlan pulled open the door.

Three small bundles tumbled across our feet.

I picked one up and kissed her on the nose—Haley.

Rose and Harry were busy pulling on Harlan's shoelaces.

"They got so excited when we pulled into your driveway," Patrick said.

"They wouldn't stay on my lap," Tyler added as he wrapped his arms around his stomach.

Harlan stepped back. "Come in."

"We won't stay long," Patrick said. In his arms a stack of puppy beds, blankets, and toys. He set everything down on the chair near the fireplace. "That's all their stuff."

"I kept a few of their toys," Tyler said, his voice low and subdued. There were tears in his eyes. He clung to Patrick's arm and set his head on Patrick's shoulder. "Can we go?"

"Do you want to say goodbye first?" Patrick replied.

Tyler shook his head. "I'd rather sneak out while they're occupied."

The pups were in the kitchen, knocking each other over, and padding around. Occasionally, barking and attacking one another. Sniffing everything. The fridge was of particular interest.

"You'll come by in a week?" I asked.

"Let's make it two," Tyler answered. "I don't want to confuse them." He sniffed and tears made tracks down his cheeks. He smiled as he watched the pups. "They'll be fine."

"We'll keep them safe," Harlan said. "Our new house will be ready in a month."

Tyler wandered over to me and wrapped his arms around my shoulders. I held him, clinging to him as we hugged. Tyler's body trembled as he cried against me.

"Thank you," I whispered to him.

"It's been a beautiful experience. Maybe I'll have my own pups someday."

"These are your pups too. You're family. Please believe that."

Tyler stepped back. "Never thought I'd be family with a rival pack."

Patrick slipped his hand into Tyler's. "Let's get you home. Get you settled in with a movie or two, and some blueberries and eggs. Tonight is going to be hard."

"For both of us," Tyler added.

Patrick sighed, tears lining his eyes. "It's true. I'm going to miss the little ruffians."

Tyler tugged on Patrick's hand and led him out through the doorway. "Take me home."

We watched them until they disappeared into the trees. We had to bundle up the three pups and take them back inside. They had tried to follow Tyler and Patrick.

When we closed the door, they whined and scratched at it for almost an hour until they got tired and fell asleep where they stood. We lifted them and put them on the bed with Reese.

They squirmed around until they incorporated Reese into their sleeping pile-up.

They would be fine. They would always have a strong bond with Tyler and Patrick and that familial relationship was what we wanted for them.

Surrounded by love.

Like Harlan and me.

Two Alphas in love.

Did you love this story? Do you want to read about Declan and his love story?

Look for ***Declan's Omegas*** by JT Fader
An MMM Wolf Shifter MPreg Romance

About the Author

JT Fader is an alternate pen name for Leigh Jarrett (she/he), allowing Leigh to explore their love of MM+ paranormal and fantasy stories by creating their own worlds.

In their hometown of Victoria, BC, Canada, Leigh can be found nestled up with their fabulously supportive wife and trusty laptop or enjoying the wondrous Vancouver Island outdoors.

To stay up to date with JT Fader's new releases and promos, check out their JT Fader Fantasticals website at www.jtfader.com.

You can also find Leigh on Bluesky.

www.ingramcontent.com/pod-product-compliance
Lightning Source LLC
Chambersburg PA
CBHW052207170626
46812CB00004B/1683